EVERYTHING THAT
Glitters

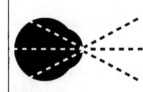

This Large Print Book carries the
Seal of Approval of N.A.V.H.

EVERYTHING THAT
Glitters

Cynthia VanRooy

Thorndike Press • Waterville, Maine

Library of Congress Cataloging-in-Publication Data

VanRooy, Cynthia.
    Everything that glitters / by Cynthia VanRooy.
        p. cm. — (Thorndike Press large print romance)
    ISBN 0-7862-7455-7 (lg. print : hc : alk. paper)
    1. Antique dealers — Fiction.   2. New Orleans (La.) —
Fiction.   3. Undercover operations — Fiction.
4. Archaeological thefts — Fiction.   5. Large type books.
I. Title.   II. Thorndike Press large print romance series.
PS3572.A673E95 2005
    813'.6—dc22   2004029992

To THEA
for the support, counsel,
and champagne

National Association for Visually Handicapped
------------------------- *serving the partially seeing*

As the Founder/CEO of NAVH, the only national health agency solely devoted to those who, although not totally blind, have an eye disease which could lead to serious visual impairment, I am pleased to recognize Thorndike Press★ as one of the leading publishers in the large print field.

Founded in 1954 in San Francisco to prepare large print textbooks for partially seeing children, NAVH became the pioneer and standard setting agency in the preparation of large type.

Today, those publishers who meet our standards carry the prestigious "Seal of Approval" indicating high quality large print. We are delighted that Thorndike Press is one of the publishers whose titles meet these standards. We are also pleased to recognize the significant contribution Thorndike Press is making in this important and growing field.

Lorraine H. Marchi, L.H.D.
Founder/CEO
NAVH

★ Thorndike Press encompasses the following imprints: Thorndike, Wheeler, Walker and Large Print Press.

Chapter One

Old World elegance greeted Greydon Cantrell when he walked through the doors of Empress Antiques. The faint scents of lemon oil and potpourri perfumed the air. He recognized the quality of the marquetry tables, the silver-green damask on the Louis XIV chairs, the giltwood mirrors. You couldn't grow up in the Cantrell family without knowing your antiques, even if as a boy you failed to regard the pieces with the respect your mother felt they were due.

Two customers monopolized the only salesperson, so Grey took the opportunity to browse through the store, studying inventory. Pale celery damask draped the wide windows across the back and sheer curtains filtered the view of the cocoa-brown waters of the Mississippi.

Paying the high-rent rates for a space on New Orleans' Riverwalk and then downplaying its most outstanding feature seemed foolish to him. He had to admit, though, the effect worked well. Being able to ignore the modern shipping traffic just yards away, shoppers could enjoy the gracious ambiance of an earlier time.

The saleswoman raised her voice, surprisingly throaty, and spoke to Grey. "I'll be with you in just a moment."

"No rush."

Grey assessed the saleswoman as he waited for her to finish with the customers. She had to be the owner. She matched her cool, serene store too well to be anything else. Champagne-blond hair was pulled back in a sleek French twist, and she wore an understated ivory suit that only hinted at the curves beneath. Pearl-droplet earrings and a narrow gold bracelet-watch were her only pieces of jewelry.

She looked too self-contained, too fastidious to involve herself in the unsavory business of smuggled antiquities. Instinctively, he wanted to discount her as a suspect, but his rational mind reminded him appearances could be deceiving. He had seen too much in his line of work to disregard the warning.

At last the customers left. The woman approached him, an impersonal smile curving her rose-tinted lips. "I'm sorry to have kept you waiting. How can I help you?"

She might have looked cool and controlled, might even have seen herself that way, but one glance into her eyes, and Grey knew otherwise. The quick flare that lighted them betrayed the fire kept ruthlessly banked behind silk and serenity. Even their color, a warm, golden caramel, tempted with the promise of rich and delicious pleasures — a promise that unfortunately he would have to pass on. For the moment.

He smiled. "I didn't mind the wait. I'd like to speak to the owner."

"I'm Jo Flaherty, the owner. What can I do for you?"

Grey reached for his wallet and pulled out his card. He hated the subterfuge, posing as a collector, but he hated more the break-up and violation of ancient cultures' remains. If he could help prevent that by making sure the people who trafficked in the illegal antiquities, who created a market for them, were stopped, he would have posed as Bozo the clown.

"I'm interested in acquiring a piece from —"

The sound of boat whistles penetrated even the insulated, climate-controlled atmosphere of the store, but Grey had tuned the noise out, so constant was the barge, tug, and ship traffic on that stretch of the

9

river. The pitch suddenly changed. Grey realized he heard warning horns, alarms.

His gaze veered to the big windows. Visible through the sheer curtains, the massive bulk of a cargo ship bore down on the mall.

"Holy — !"

At his reaction the woman looked over her shoulder and gasped. The ship loomed, darkening the store and galvanizing Grey into action.

"Move!" He grabbed her arm and all but dragged the frozen woman toward the entrance.

He yanked open the door to the mall's main corridor, pushed her out, and followed. In the hall, a surging mass of panicked Christmas shoppers attempted to escape the shopping center before the freighter hit.

Grey pulled the woman to one side, keeping her from being trampled in the rush. He worked their way along the wall as quickly as he could in the crush. The woman followed close behind him, her hand grasped firmly in his. All hell was about to break loose. He wanted them as far away as possible when it did.

The freighter crashed and the sound boomed and echoed through the mall like a bomb. The building plunged into darkness, shuddered, and began to collapse in on itself. Broken concrete, glass, and water rained down.

Grey turned and pressed the woman against the wall, shielding her with his body. A falling timber struck him hard, knocking them both to the floor.

He landed heavily on the woman, feeling something give in his shoulder. Powerless to do anything except duck his head, he closed his eyes tightly against the falling dust, debris, and shards of glass.

The destruction seemed to go on forever. When at last the noise of the imploding building quieted, Grey heard people buried in the rubble with them screaming. He didn't know which sound was worse.

The beam that had felled him lay across his back, pinning both him and the woman. He blinked to clear the dust from his eyes. Meager pinpoints of light through the wreckage were enough to show him even if he had the strength to push the beam off, they were trapped.

Amid the acrid smells of dust, wet plaster, and sparking wiring he caught the perfumed scent of the woman beneath him, like white spring flowers — jasmine, magnolia, lilacs — sheer and utterly feminine. It struck him as an insanely normal thing to notice — the fragrance of a beautiful woman — in the middle of madness.

Jo lay on her back, stunned. She attempted to draw the air back into her lungs that had been so abruptly knocked out of them. A heavy weight pressed her, making breathing more difficult than it should have to be. She frowned, trying to make sense of the situation. Confusion muddled her, before memory flooded back.

The man in the store — the one with eyes the color of a hot Louisiana summer sky — had pulled her out, had protected her while the building came apart around them. Even now his body sheltered hers, the hard, lean planes of it between her and the worst of the destruction.

Cries and sobs rose from the wreckage around them. She started to speak, but dust choked her. She coughed and tried again. "What happened?"

The words came out so faintly she wasn't sure he heard. The horrible possibility occurred that he might be injured, might not even be conscious.

When he spoke, relief left her weak. "Freighter . . . rammed the mall." His words sounded as though they came from behind clenched teeth, but at least he was conscious and coherent.

"Why?" she asked, horrified.

She could feel the slight shake of his head. "God knows. Are you all right?"

"I think so." Her voice shook. "What about you?"

"I've been better." His voice sounded strained. "Sorry I'm crushing you. I don't seem to have much choice."

She ignored his apology, more concerned with his first comment. "Where do you hurt?"

"My shoulder. I think it's dislocated."

"Is the pain bad?"

"Define bad." She could hear his teeth grinding.

"I wish there was something I could do."

"Me, too, lady, but rescuers will dig survivors out as soon as possible."

"Do you think anyone was killed?"

"It would be a miracle if they weren't."

"Oh, God." She lay incredulous, unable to take in the enormity of the disaster that didn't happen in her world. Such horror happened on the evening news, to other people. "Do you think they'll find us right away?"

"The trick will be in not dislodging this precarious pile of rubble and making things worse."

Jo hadn't thought of that. She wished he hadn't. The cries around them rose in volume. Bits of debris rattled through the maze. Her breath caught in a sudden attack of claustrophobia. Her skin prickled and perspiration broke out in spite of the damp winter chill making itself felt. A timber groaned close by, sending her pulse rate soaring. They were going to die.

"We have to get out! Now!" She bucked, trying to throw off the weight that pinned her. Panic lent her strength as she pushed at the beam imprisoning them.

"Jo! Isn't that what you said your name was? Stop! Just stop. All you're going to do is exhaust yourself."

His level voice restored a measure of reason to her, but her heart still beat wildly.

"Take a long slow breath and concentrate on calming down."

His firm, steady words, spoken into her ear, centered her and gave her back control.

"I'm sorry. I've got a grip now. It won't happen again."

At least she hoped it wouldn't. God only knew how long they'd have to lie there before help came.

What would she have done if Prince Charming hadn't shown up? She already thought of him in those terms. During her unhappy childhood, she had dreamed of a Prince Charming like the one in her favorite story. He would ride into her life and rescue her, carry her away to a better place where they would live happily ever after. Her rescuer even looked like one of the illustrations in her book, with his blue eyes, hair the color of chicory coffee, and strong jaw.

In their forced embrace, her hand rested at the back of his neck. At first she thought the wetness under her fingers was water. It had sprayed everywhere, thrown up by the impact of the ship. She rubbed her fingers together testingly. The liquid was too viscous for water. She tunneled her fingers under his thick hair, exploring the back of his skull carefully.

"I'm assuming you're not coming on to me," he said, "so what the hell are you doing?"

"Something must have hit your head. There's blood back here. I'm looking for an injury."

He grunted. "You just found it."

Her hand had discovered the area slightly to one side where his hair matted damply. Blood still seeped slowly from the broken skin, and she felt where a bump

15

was forming. "Does it hurt?"

"It didn't until you called my attention to it."

She was instantly contrite. "I'm sorry. I was worried."

"There is something you can do."

"What?"

"Talk."

"I don't understand."

"Talk to me. It'll help distract both of us."

She swallowed, knowing he had a greater need for distraction than she did. "What should I talk about?"

"Anything. Why did you call your store Empress Antiques?"

She closed her eyes, concentrated on relaxing her body against the latent panic that still lurked at the edges of her consciousness, and let herself go back in memory.

As a child, she had been shuffled from foster home to foster home, school to school so often, being the new kid was the norm for her. As a defense against the vulnerability of it, she had developed an aloofness many saw as snobbishness. In high school history when they learned about Napoleon and Josephine, the other kids taunted her with the title Empress.

"My full name is Josephine," she told

him. It had given her grim satisfaction to turn the taunt into something to be proud of.

"Clever. Uncommon name these days."

"I was born on March fourteenth."

"Ah. St. Joseph's Day."

She knew him then for a New Orleans native. In a city where the diverse mix of cultures gave rise to more than the usual excuses to party, St. Joseph's Day was celebrated with enthusiasm. She never knew whether her mother had named her after the patron saint of families in a bout of wishful thinking or as a cynical joke.

Jo and the woman who had given birth to her in prison had never become well acquainted. Her mother refused to sign a release making Jo adoptable, condemning her to a series of foster homes. By the time her mother died, Jo was thirteen and no one wanted to adopt an adolescent. She tried not to harbor bitterness toward the young woman who couldn't give her a home and wouldn't let anyone else do so, but it was difficult.

"In business long?"

"A few years."

"You seem too young for such success."

"Twenty-nine?" She felt old enough to have lived two lifetimes. "Maybe. But most people don't work as hard as I do."

Most people had lives with broader horizons. Hers had narrowed to insuring she would never be dependent on anyone else again. She had done that. She hadn't meant to let the need consume all her energies, but it had done so just the same.

"Whoever said women talk a lot, never met you, lady," his gritty voice commented. "Come on, help me out here. Husband, boyfriend, engaged?"

"Sorry. None of the above." She hadn't had time — or hadn't been willing to spend the time cultivating a truly deep relationship.

The irony of her situation was that her greatest desire was for a husband and family of her own, the family she never had. Perhaps she had assumed one would just appear when the time was right. After her last birthday she had decided the time was right. She was still waiting.

She thought she heard the man mutter a curse. It was hard to be sure in the awful cacophony of cries. "I . . . I could tell you about my customers. Some funny things happen in the business."

"Fine. Whatever. Just talk . . . please."

She talked. She told him every story she could think of, elaborating and exaggerating when necessary to make the telling more interesting. He became so still she thought he might have passed out, but when she stopped talking he urged her to continue.

At one point, the wreckage settled noisily again, and she caught her breath in fear.

"It's all right. It's okay," he reassured her, even as he spoke through his teeth.

She exhaled a shuddering breath, clinging desperately to the sound of his voice. His body covering hers gave her a sense of comfort, ineffectual barrier though it would be if the building collapsed further. One of her arms was around his neck in the parody of a more personal embrace. Although, she considered, facing possible death together was about as personal as you could get.

"Go on. Mrs. LeMay wanted the armoire you had already promised to . . ."

With an effort, she dragged her mind away from the unstable pile around them. When she had exhausted the topic of her shop, she went back to college. She told him about going to Sophie Newcomb on a partial scholarship. Earning the scholarship had been easy. Having few friends in high school gave her plenty of time for studies.

19

She talked about working part-time as a clerk in an antique store to pay her living expenses and how she had fallen in love with the beautiful furniture, the pieces that had a presence and history. The last was especially appealing to her. Unless she counted an unwed mother doing time for the armed robbery her boyfriend had bullied her into, she had no family, no history of her own. She refrained from sharing the story of her mother with him, kept the shame to herself.

"College boyfriends?"

She smiled slightly. "A few."

He shifted and she heard him bite back a moan. "Tell me."

"You know. The usual."

"Boyfriends is not a topic I'm well-versed in."

Feeling him draw a careful breath, she hurt for him and hurried to take his mind off the pain. "The first college boy I dated was the sensitive-poet type — you know, ascetic, bearded, with a misunderstood soul. After a while, I tired of being his audience. He moved on to someone with more sensitivity."

She thought she felt him smile against her temple. "And then?"

"Then I dated a jock. When he could fit

me in between practices. I never worried about another girl. He wouldn't have had time."

"What happened to *him?*"

"I got tired of sitting in the bleachers. They weren't that comfortable."

"So he was replaced by . . . ?"

"A physics major. We dated until he figured out I didn't really understand half of what he said. I had just been smiling and faking it."

The sound of amusement that rumbled in his throat pleased her immensely. She had succeeded for a few minutes in bringing him relief.

"Which one was the first?"

Her heart stumbled. "The first what?" she stalled.

"The first time you had sex. Which guy?"

She licked her lips and tasted grit. "None of them."

"None?"

"My first time was in high school."

"How old were you?"

She hadn't thought about it in years. Had tried hard not to. "Seventeen. I'd rather talk about something else."

"Later. This is interesting. Steady boyfriend?"

"No." If she harbored any hope her curt tone would discourage him, he quashed it.

"I don't get it. Explain."

She shifted uncomfortably and heard his sharp inhalation. She froze immediately and muttered an apology. Instinctively she knew he wouldn't feel his own physical pain as much if he could concentrate on her old emotional one.

"I was new to the school, didn't know many of the students," she said. "He was popular, part of the 'in' crowd. I was so thrilled when he asked me out. On our third date he told me we were going to a party, we were going to have some real fun." She paused, remembering the details of that night like it was the previous week.

"What happened?" His tone registered suspicion, as though he could already discern the outcome.

"He drove me out of town to the bayou. After he parked the car, I asked where the party was. He said it was later, he wanted to have a drink first. He opened a couple of Cokes and then spiked them with rum from a flask he pulled out from under the front seat."

Her voice quavered and she took a steadying breath. "I didn't like the way it tasted, so I only sipped mine. He drank his right away. He said if I wasn't going to have my drink, there was no point in waiting. Then he kissed me and started pawing at me." She stopped, squeezing her eyes shut against the image of her date that night.

"Finish it," he said, voice grim.

"When I tried to push him away, to get out of the car, he slapped me. It made him mad that I didn't want to have sex with him. He told me that it was going to happen anyway, so I might just as well relax and enjoy it. I begged him not to, I tried to fight him, but he was bigger.

"When it was over, he zipped his jeans, started the car, and drove me home like everything was perfectly normal. He said it would be stupid for me to tell anybody, because no one would believe I hadn't wanted it. He would make sure of that. When I got out of the car, he even asked if I wanted to go out the next week."

That had been the worst part. The humiliation of his thinking she would let herself be treated that way. She remembered sneaking into the house, hiding her ruined panties under trash in the garbage can so her foster mother wouldn't find them, wouldn't ask questions.

"You were a virgin?"

"Yes." Her voice was flat, betraying none of the anguish, the heartbreak of that night.

He growled an obscenity. "I'm sorry, Jo. You make me ashamed of fifty percent of the human race. Did you report the bastard?"

"No. He was right. No one would have believed me. I was new, we *had* been going out, and he came from a 'fine old family.'"

She had never told anyone. She had been so ashamed of her naiveté, too afraid she wouldn't be believed. She suddenly realized those were the feelings of the seventeen-year-old girl she had been, not the woman she had become. Because she hadn't been willing to think about that night, she hadn't been able to move beyond it.

Amazingly, she could already feel herself letting it go. The telling had been painful, but it was like lancing a boil. The poison could finally drain away. If they survived, she would be grateful to the stranger for the rest of her life.

"No one's family is fine enough or old enough to justify rape," he said. "If that had happened to either one of my sisters, I'd have insured the guy was half-dead before I let the police have him."

She tried to imagine what it would be

like having a brother, having anyone who stood up for you, helped you fight your battles. Whatever she had achieved or accomplished, she had done on her own.

"A brother is a luxury I don't have."

"No siblings?"

"No." No anything.

"Why were you new?"

"I moved a lot, then." She had opened herself up enough. Healing as it might have been, she needed a respite. "Tell me about your sisters."

"Andrea's a doctor in Baton Rouge. Sarah works as an interior designer here."

"Married?"

"Me or them?"

She didn't care one way or the other about his sisters, but it mattered very much to her whether he was single. "Either, all."

"Sarah's still single. Andrea's married. I'm currently unattached."

"Currently?"

"Divorced."

"Kids?"

"No. Didn't make that mistake."

"You think having kids is a mistake?" she asked, disappointed.

"With my ex-wife, yes."

"What was she like?"

"A bitch."

His tone didn't encourage further questions, and Jo fell silent. She wondered how long they had been lying there. The floor beneath her was cold, and if not for the man on top of her, she would have been chilled clear through. She raised her arm to look at her watch over his shoulder, but couldn't make out the numbers in the meager light. The voices around them had quieted disturbingly.

She closed her eyes, exhausted by the emotional gamut she had run. Unlikely as she would have thought the possibility, she felt herself drifting into a sleepy daze, and noted in a distant corner of her mind the pleasant woodsy scent of the man's aftershave. Minutes or hours later she heard new voices — strong ones, calling, hailing anyone who might be trapped in their area. She came alert instantly, hope surging through her.

"Rescue workers," her companion mumbled.

She frowned at the faint timbre of the voice she had already come to know as firm and assured. The man needed medical help and soon. She answered the calls, raising her voice as loudly as she could. The workers responded, assuring her they would have them out as quickly as possible.

She felt the muscles under her hand go lax, and the man instantly grew heavier. He had finally passed out. She was so worried for him, so anxious about his care, the last hour seemed twice as long as those that preceded it. Jo held onto her patience with difficulty as the workers dug and shifted concrete gingerly, not wanting to hurry and worsen the situation.

At last the rescuers were lifting the timber that had held them down.

"Be careful of his shoulder," Jo cautioned them, before they lifted the man off her. "He said he thought it was dislocated."

One of the medics lifting him to a stretcher glanced at it. "Looks like it might be."

"Also, there's a wound on the back of his head."

"We'll take care of it."

Rescuers assisted her to an aid station that had been set up, and wrapped her in a blanket. The man who had been with her, they loaded into an ambulance. She tried to protest that she wanted to stay with him, but when the medics realized he was a stranger to her, her words were dismissed as hysteria. Before she could make herself understood, the ambulance pulled away from the scene.

Thanks to her Prince Charming she had escaped any injuries except bruises. He hadn't been so lucky. She thought about their hours in the darkness together, what it would have been like if she had been alone. Even uninjured, she wasn't sure she could have survived the fear. He had kept her sane.

And she didn't even know his name.

Chapter Two

Grey accepted the dry martini on the rocks from his aunt, Vivian Duvalier, and settled back in the wing chair. "Thanks." He sipped, enjoying the taste of the sharp, icy liquid for a moment before swallowing. "Perfect, as usual."

"You look tired, Grey. I know the end of the semester is always a busy time for you."

His position as a professor of anthropology lent authenticity to his claim of an interest in the old artifacts. It also gave him the cover he needed in his other work. The Customs Service had recruited him years earlier as an undercover agent because of his expertise on the cultures of the Middle East and North Africa.

"Yes, it's the usual pre-holiday crunch." The university classes he taught were winding up the semester and he had been administering final exams. He felt more than ready to just sit and relax for a while. The past week and a half he had had time to do neither.

After a day in the hospital, he picked up

the investigation he had been working on where he left off, with Jo Flaherty. This time, though, the focus was different. Rather than looking for a suspect, he had been attempting to prove, to himself and Customs, that Jo was in no way involved with the recent smuggling of illegal artifacts from Mali into the United States.

Although he had found no evidence to implicate her, unhappily he had turned up both motive and opportunity. He knew why Jo had been new to the high school she talked about, knew about her being shuffled from one foster home to another, knew about the mother who had died of pneumonia in prison.

While he sympathized with the child she had been, he reminded himself that avoidance of poverty would be a strong motivator for the adult she had become. That kind of upbringing had to have left its mark. He just didn't know what it was yet. But he would find out.

Jo received shipments arriving in New Orleans via the Mississippi from all over the world. The bill of lading listed the contents, and inspections by Customs was usually cursory. It would be an easy matter to hide a small object inside something larger, like a cushion.

If things with Customs got too hot, there was always the bayou. In a tradition that went back over two hundred years, contraband could be taken off the ship in secret and hidden in that maze of waterways for as long as necessary.

Of course, Jo's situation wasn't unique. Any dealer could avail himself of the same opportunity. That was one of the reasons the investigation was so painstaking. He took another sip and leaned his head wearily against the back of the chair.

"All right, Grey, what is this about?"

He lifted his head and looked at his aunt, who had seated herself in a matching chair across from him. Her feathery cap of red hair had faded to strawberry blond and laugh lines fanned out from the corners of her eyes, but she held her fifty-plus years well. At the moment, blue eyes almost the same shade as his gazed at him shrewdly.

At his questioning expression, she said, "I gave up years ago trying to fix you up. You as much as said your love life was none of my business. Now here you are insisting I invite Jo for dinner. And don't give me that story about 'just wanting to get to know her.' I'm not buying it. You've never wanted to get to know one of my friends before."

When Vivian had mentioned a new friend she had met through one of her charity committees who was in the antique business, he had paid only scant attention. After the accident at Riverwalk, Vivian had been horrified for her friend, whose business had been wiped out. She said Jo Flaherty was fortunate not to have been killed, because she had been in her store at the time of the accident. Jo credited a man who had been with her, whose name she never found out, with saving her.

The accident had been the main topic of everyone's conversation for several days after the accident. Terrorism, the first thing that came to mind those days, had been ruled out and the cause was discovered to be a garden-variety malfunction in the ship's steering mechanism. Grey hadn't volunteered the information that he was the man her friend spoke about. Vivian had no idea he had been anywhere near Riverwalk when the accident occurred. Although she treated their relationship casually, he knew the depth of love his aunt felt for him. He had thought to spare her by not telling her. However, the news of Vivian's friendship with Jo had been too good an opportunity for Grey to pass up.

Although she was bound to be upset

when she learned of his part in the accident, Grey hoped that seeing him currently alive and well would help to mitigate her feelings. That she would be annoyed he hadn't told her earlier, was a given. Annoyance he could easily cajole her out of. He had been doing it all his life.

His aunt sipped her martini and regarded him steadily, waiting for an explanation of his uncharacteristic interest. He rolled his head on the chair back tiredly toward her. "If I promise you'll understand when Jo gets here, will you wait?"

"Do I have a choice, or are you just being polite?"

A corner of his mouth slanted up. "Just being polite, I'm afraid. How long are you in town for?"

Vivian spent as much time traveling as she did in her Garden District home. Widowed early in her marriage and childless, she had few responsibilities to keep her tied down. She took advantage of the freedom, flying off to whatever exotic location took her fancy.

Grey reflected that it must be something in the Cantrell blood. He liked nothing better than working on a dig in some remote area. Rich northerners rented the home he grew up in a block away while his parents sailed on a round-the-world cruise.

Vivian studied him a moment in silence, then allowed him his change of subject. "I'm leaving for Key West in a couple of months. I'll be back, though, before the weather there gets hot and sticky. If I want hot and sticky I can stay home and have it for free."

The doorbell rang. At Grey's sudden tensing, she shot him a look of interest and rose to answer it. He heard Vivian greet Jo in the entrance hall, heard the soft voice he remembered answer her. He set his drink on a side table and stood.

The women entered the room, Vivian explaining that her nephew was joining them for dinner. Jo glanced up, a socially polite smile curving her mouth. The trim silk suit he had last seen her in had been replaced by narrow wool slacks in a soft cream and a matching tunic-style sweater that skimmed the curves beneath it. An antique gold locket suspended from a chain hung below her breasts, the "V" it formed drawing his gaze down her body.

He forcibly dragged his focus back up to her face, framed by a silver-gold fall of hair, longer than he had suspected. He had been right about her eyes. They made him think of hot caramel sauce over cool vanilla ice cream.

At the sight of him, those eyes widened and warmed with her smile. "Prince Charming!" She turned to Vivian, her smile wide. "This is your nephew?"

"Yes," Vivian replied in surprise. "Do you two know each other?"

"Do we ever," Jo answered. She moved forward and took Grey's hands, clasping them warmly. "You don't know how glad I am to finally find you and see you looking so well," she told him.

If she felt shy or embarrassed about the things she had told him during their time together, she hid the signs well. Grey didn't think anyone was that good an actress. His gut tightened at the instant attraction he felt to her. He had thought it was imagination, had chalked it up to heightened emotions during the accident, but his memory hadn't played him false. That mysterious connection he had felt between them from the first moment he looked into her eyes was still there.

"Prince Charming?" he asked.

A blush tinted her cheeks. "I never learned your name. In my mind, I had to call you something." A delicate shrug lifted one shoulder.

He grinned. "I've been called worse."

"I tried to find you afterwards. No one I

spoke to knew which hospital you had been taken to. Since all I had was a physical description, no name, people couldn't help me much. I even tried calling the hospitals myself. You wouldn't believe how tight-lipped admissions can be."

Her expression reflected her impatience with the bureaucracy. "I had just about given up ever being able to tell you how grateful I am for your help."

Grey was spared having to answer by his aunt's interruption. "Hospital? Grey, what does she mean?"

Jo turned to Vivian, her surprise evident. "He was the man with me in the accident. I don't know what I would have done without him. Didn't he tell you?"

Vivian pinned her nephew with a look that promised retribution. "No, he didn't say a word."

"He was even hurt protecting me."

Grey winced at the small cry that issued from Vivian. Jo's assessing gaze traveled over him quickly. "How's your shoulder?" she asked.

"It's fine. The doctors popped it back into place and I was good as new." No point in telling her it still ached if he moved wrong.

"And your head?" She reached up and

ran her fingers lightly over the area that had been injured. As her hand cupped the back of his head, she appeared to realize her actions might be considered unorthodox. Her gaze flew to his, then slid away awkwardly as she drew her hand back.

He understood why touching him had come naturally to her. She hadn't hesitated until she thought about it. He understood because he was wrestling with the same kind of feelings.

Their relationship seemed to have been condensed by the experience they had shared. They had already bypassed the social barriers that usually required time and acquaintance to hurdle. He felt closer to her after a few hours than women he had known for several years.

He stifled the urge to grasp the hand she pulled away and cleared his throat. "Stitches came out two days ago."

"Stitches!" Vivian's eyes grew large and her complexion paled. "I need to sit down." She did so, sinking weakly into the nearest chair.

Grey was grateful for the distraction. Jo's gentle touch had fired off nerves that had no business reacting to the purely platonic concern.

He reached for his aunt's drink and

handed it to her. "Here. This is why I didn't tell you. There wasn't a damn thing you could do, so it seemed stupid to upset you. I'm sorry you had to find out."

"Well, I'm not." Vivian was beginning to rally. Her color improved. Her eyes promised him they would talk more later, before settling on Jo with a speculative gleam. "I want to hear everything about it."

"Wait," Jo said. "I *have* to know something first."

Grey looked at her, his brows arched. "What?"

"What *is* your name?"

He gave a bark of laughter. "Greydon Cantrell," he told her, sweeping a bow, before straightening with a smile. "Call me Grey. Before Vivian starts her inquisition can I offer you a drink?"

"A glass of white wine?"

"No problem." He left the room, returning minutes later with Jo's drink. He handed it to her and took his seat across from the two women. "All right, Viv, I think we're ready. Fire away and let's get this over with." His wink at Jo had his aunt pressing her lips together in mock sternness.

Grey and Jo filled Vivian in on all the details of the accident, answering questions until at last Vivian's curiosity was satisfied. They discussed how amazing it was that no one had been killed, truly a Christmas miracle.

Vivian's gaze went from Jo to her nephew and he could almost see the wheels turning. "How fortunate for each of you to have had the other."

Grey slanted his aunt a look, but couldn't be irritated at her remark, not when he agreed with it.

"Having Grey in the store at just that moment was a gift," Jo said.

"Why *were* you shopping in an antique store, Grey?" Vivian asked. "You've never professed an interest before."

"I ran an errand at Riverwalk and had a little extra time. The place looked intriguing."

Jo frowned at him, but said nothing.

"And now that pretty shop is just kindling," the older woman said regretfully. "I hope you're going to reopen somewhere soon."

Jo told them about her search for a new location. She had called her insurance company immediately and didn't expect any problems. She described an empty store on Magazine Street that she was considering. Several other antique businesses operated nearby, so the right clientele would already be in the neighborhood.

"Besides, I like the two big old live oak trees that shelter the front." Her smile acknowledged the less-than-businesslike reason for her decision.

"The older area will provide a better ambiance for your business, anyway," Vivian said, sounding determined to find a bright side to the disaster.

"That's true," Jo agreed. "I'm so glad that if something like this had to happen, at least the only thing damaged was new construction, not part of New Orleans' history."

"Isn't that the truth?" Vivian said.

"I'd be at a loss if the old Cafe du Monde had been destroyed," Jo said. "I've been reading the newspaper there every Sunday morning since I moved into the Quarter eight years ago. It would be a shock to my system if I had to read about the week's happenings somewhere else."

"Coffee and beignets make even the worst headlines easier to take. Are you going to keep the same name for the shop when you reopen?"

"Of course. I've already built up a good clientele and reputation. I intend to maintain that." The women continued to chat about Jo's store and the time frame for its reopening.

Grey took mental notes while Jo talked,

admitting to himself that his interest was as much personal as professional. He remembered too well the feel of her body beneath his. He intended to have it there again, under vastly different circumstances.

"Grey? I asked what you'd heard from your parents."

"What? Sorry, Viv. My mind must have wandered." No doubt about it. "I got a letter a couple of weeks ago. They were in Valparaiso, Chile getting ready for a side trip inland. Having a great time, as usual."

"Good. I do miss them, though. My brother and his wife," she explained in an aside to Jo. "You'd like them. Nice people." She turned back to Grey. "By the time they return, I'll be gone. Sometimes it feels like this family is as scattered as buckshot. When's the last time we all got together?"

"Christmas two years ago? No, Andrea was doing her residency at Johns Hopkins and couldn't get away. It was three years ago."

"Much too long. We must plan something soon."

Grey made a noncommittal noise. He could never predict more than two weeks into the future what his schedule would look like.

Jo listened to the conversation between

41

Grey and Vivian, unable to comprehend having family you loved, were connected to, and not making every effort to be with them. Only people who had always had family could afford the luxury of taking them for granted. The same went for money and security.

She considered her feelings about Vivian's home. It was beautiful, filled with valuable antiques that Jo had tried more than once to buy for the store. Vivian had laughed and said her ancestors would come back to haunt her if she sold off so much as a teaspoon.

Jo didn't envy the things in Vivian's home or even the lovely Italianate building in which she lived. Her own historic house in the French Quarter was every bit as gracious, furnished with items from around the world as beautiful as anything Vivian owned. What she envied was Vivian's refusal to be intimidated by any of it. The draperies at the windows were faded from the sunlight and the upholstery on the priceless French chairs was comfortably worn.

Jo doubted she would ever reach the stage of being able to rest her feet on a footstool without first kicking off her shoes, or casually drop her sterling silver into the dishwasher, rather than washing it lovingly by hand. She had worked too hard for what she had, and lived too long without beauty around her to ever take even the smallest bit of it for granted.

"That reminds me," Vivian said. "Jo, have you made plans for Christmas, yet?"

Jo had told Vivian a little of her background, about the foster families. When Vivian asked about her parents, she had said simply that they were dead. She actually had no idea whether her father was or not. She hoped so.

"I thought I'd relax, take it easy. Things will be so hectic with making arrangements to open the new store, I'm going to give myself that day off."

"You must spend it with us. Grey's sister Sarah will be here and maybe Andrea, depending on her hospital schedule."

"I don't want to intrude on a private family day."

"Nonsense. We'd love to have you. With the close call you and Grey had we have an extra reason to celebrate. It will be more special with you here. You must come," Vivian pronounced. "Tell her, Grey."

He grinned lopsidedly. "You've been doing a pretty good job." His smile grew more serious when he turned to Jo.

43

"Vivian's words go for me, too. I'd like you to be here. Please."

Her reservations dissolved in the warmth of his blue eyes. In that tone of voice, he could have asked for almost anything and she would have granted it gladly. "Thank you, I'd like that, too. What can I bring?" she asked Vivian.

"Nothing, just yourself and a party mood. Now, let's have dinner."

Over a delicious meal of fresh catfish, Jo asked Grey what he did for a living.

"I'm an anthropology professor at Tulane."

His answer surprised her. With his athletic physique and commanding presence, he was the most unlikely college professor she had ever encountered. If there had been anthropology professors like Grey when she attended college, she certainly didn't remember them. She might have majored in something other than business.

"Do you enjoy it?" she asked.

"I wouldn't do it if I didn't." Jo received the impression Grey did very little that he didn't want to do.

"What do you like best about it?"

"Hooking a student's interest, curiosity. Most of them come into my classes just to fill a requirement and hope they can do it

44

as painlessly as possible. I'm almost addicted to the thrill I get when I see them become awed by another culture. It's important that they realize their own culture, their own society is not necessarily the best just because it's theirs. Learning begins with humility, and no one is cockier than a college student."

"Grey, dear, come down," Vivian admonished. "You're on your soapbox again."

His smile flashed at Jo apologetically. "Sorry. Vivian's right. It's an occupational hazard."

"Don't apologize," Jo said. "I happen to agree with you. One of the things I love about my business is learning about the things produced by a society to meet its needs. The methods used to make those items beautiful are fascinating studying. For instance, in seventeenth century France —"

"Not you, too!" Vivian's expression was comical.

Grey laughed. "Vivian can only take what I do in small doses. Relax, Vivian. Jo and I will get together privately."

The look he sent Jo guaranteed more than shop talk. Their gazes locked over the table in a bond she couldn't begin to understand or explain.

Later, as Jo savored the dessert of chocolate mousse, calories she didn't usually allow herself, she heard the beginning notes of Beethoven's Fifth.

"Good Heavens," Vivian said. "What's that?"

"My cell phone," Grey muttered, leaning back in his chair and reaching into the pocket of his slacks. He withdrew the instrument, flipped it open, and glanced at the number displayed. His expression became serious.

"I need to answer this. Excuse me." He stood, laying his napkin on the table, and strode quickly into the kitchen.

"What in the world?" Vivian asked of the room at large. She blinked at the door he had walked through. "That's never happened before."

Jo spooned up a mouthful of dessert, telling herself she wasn't really trying to eavesdrop on Grey's conversation. His voice could be heard from the kitchen, the tone curt and serious, but she couldn't distinguish words. She felt oddly disquieted. Grey had told Vivian he had been killing time in Jo's store, but she remembered his words that day clearly. He had said he was interested in a particular piece.

Grey returned a short time later and

went to his aunt's chair. "Vivian, I'm sorry. I have to leave now. There's a problem I need to handle." He bent and placed a kiss on the top of her head. "Don't get up. I'll call you in the morning." He straightened. "Walk me to the door, Jo?"

"Of course," she answered, mystified. Grey came around the table and pulled out her chair, then directed her with his hand at the back of her waist.

In the foyer Jo turned to him, curious. She found him staring down at her, a look in his eyes she couldn't interpret. "Grey?"

"This is not the way I wanted the evening to end. You know I have to see you again."

Then he felt it too, the indefinable connection between them. "Yes." Her voice came out barely louder than a whisper.

Meeting his gaze, she felt heated by his summer-blue eyes, and her breath caught. He was going to kiss her. Dread tightened her stomach.

Chapter Three

Grey lifted a hand and cupped the side of Jo's neck, his thumb gently tilting her chin up. She stood perfectly still, watching him with wide eyes. He started to lower his head, then checked the movement. Something was not quite right. He seemed to be receiving mixed signals from her.

All evening he had felt the sexual awareness vibrating between them, had had all he could do not to drag her out of Vivian's and take her on the first horizontal surface that presented itself. Every look she directed at him had been an invitation, whether she realized it or not.

Now she stood passively, hands at her sides, waiting for him to act. She made no move herself to welcome the kiss, or even participate. He could swear she was holding her breath.

He frowned, studying her face. Was she frightened? He didn't think so. Her stillness wasn't a cowering one. He had the sudden impression she was humoring him, that she was willing to let him kiss her, but had no interest herself.

His eyes narrowed. They'd see about that. He lowered his head until their mouths were only a breath apart, then paused. He felt her small inhalation of surprise, before she raised her face the fraction of an inch necessary to allow their mouths to meet.

He let their lips brush, nothing more, before touching her mouth again, lingering a second longer. When he pressed it a third time, her lips remained closed and impassive, but he felt her jaw shift under his hand slightly, bringing her mouth more firmly against his.

He didn't attempt to pull her closer, didn't try to deepen the kiss, simply held her lightly with a hand on her neck. He forced himself to keep the kiss gentle, though what he wanted to do was back her against the nearest wall and imprint his body on hers.

He was rewarded for his patience when her lips softened beneath his. He broke off the kiss immediately and straightened. Her eyes opened in puzzlement.

His hand kept her face tipped up to his. "We're going to talk about what just happened here the next time I see you," he warned. Her gaze dropped, and he wondered what thoughts she masked.

He glanced at his watch, frustrated he didn't have time to deal with the issue at the moment. They were going to get things out in the open at the earliest opportunity. He released her and reached for the door-knob.

"I've got to go. You'd better get back to Vivian before the curiosity kills her. Sorry to leave you to handle it. If all else fails, tell her to mind her own business." He flashed a quick smile and winked, before opening the door.

Jo stood in the foyer after he left, using a moment to gather her thoughts before re-joining Vivian. What *had* just happened? She had been afraid she would feel nothing, had been prepared to feel nothing. As usual. Instead, the first faint stirrings of something she was afraid to call desire had quickened in her blood.

She cherished the fragile, nascent excitement, holding the knowledge of it to her breast hopefully.

"Jo?"

She looked up to find Vivian standing in the dining room doorway.

"I heard Grey leave," Vivian said. "When you didn't come back I became concerned."

"I'm sorry. I was just thinking."

50

Vivian arched a brow. "Must have been interesting thoughts."

Vivian's brow arched higher at the flush Jo felt warm her cheeks, but mercifully the woman refrained from commenting on it. "Shall we have our coffee in the living room?" she asked instead.

They settled in front of the fire that burned cozily, banishing the damp December chill. Vivian poured for each of them, then lifted her own cup and sipped. She replaced the cup on the saucer that rested on her lap. "Grey's behavior was unusual. I can't imagine what kind of an emergency an anthropology professor could possibly have," she commented. "That's never happened before."

"Maybe a problem with one of his students," Jo suggested.

"Hmm." Vivian's expression remained skeptical.

"He did say he'd call you tomorrow. Perhaps he'll be able to explain then."

"I hope so." Vivian tipped her head. "In any case, I wanted to tell you how pleased I am that you and Grey have met. I'm sorry, though, that the circumstances were so awful. You are just what Grey has needed. You would be so good for him." A shadow crossed her face. "I'm just not sure he would be so good for you."

"Why would you say something like that?" Jo asked, trying not to feel hurt by Vivian's comment.

"I like you very much, Jo. I would hate to see you hurt. I'm afraid Grey could do that without meaning to."

"In what way?"

"Grey was married once."

"I know. He told me while we were waiting for help."

"How much did he say?"

"Just enough to imply it hadn't been a happy marriage."

Vivian gave an unladylike snort. "That's an understatement. Missy Squire's father lost a fortune to a gambling habit. In the process, he also lost the family home. The scandal liked to have killed Missy. Grey had had a thing for her for years. Well, she came on to him in a big way, and he fell completely. He was young and idealistic and thought she loved him as much as he loved her."

Vivian tsked disgustedly. "The flowers in her wedding bouquet had barely wilted before she made it plain she had only married him to assure herself of a place in society. Grey should have dumped her right then and there, but he felt honor-bound to make the best of the marriage. That little shrew started running through his money like he was printing it in the basement. Grey never said much, but I know they fought about it a lot."

Jo felt uncomfortable discussing Grey behind his back, but couldn't prevent herself from asking, "What happened?"

Vivian's face registered her disdain for Grey's ex-wife. "Grey came home in the middle of the afternoon and caught her with the pool man, who was servicing something other than the apartment swimming pool. Grey was willing to tolerate a lot of things from her, but infidelity was *not* among them. He settled more on her than she had a right to expect and has barely spoken of her since."

"He must have been devastated."

"Yes, he was," Vivian said quietly. "He's been with women since, but I don't believe he's let a one touch his heart. I don't know that he ever will again. I love Grey dearly, but not blindly. I know he's hurt women who cared too much for him. That's why I worry about you. He needs someone like you, but I'd hate to see him hurt you."

The woman's honesty touched Jo. She leaned forward and grasped Vivian's hand. "I appreciate your care, but Grey and I have just met. I think it's premature to be concerned."

Vivian turned her hand over and returned Jo's clasp. "I don't. I saw the two of you tonight. Grey wants you. And I got the distinct impression you wouldn't find his attention unwelcome."

Jo looked away for a moment, annoyed to feel a flush creep up her neck. She forced herself to meet Vivian's gaze. "I would like to see him again, true. Beyond that . . . I don't know. We'll see."

Vivian studied Jo. "You don't go out much, do you?"

"I'm usually too busy. There hasn't been an opportunity to meet many men." Jo picked at nonexistent lint on her sweater and avoided Vivian's eyes.

"On second thought," Vivian said, "Grey may be just what you need. If you're not careful, you could turn into one of those bloodless, all-business kind of women. Nothing like a blazing affair to remind you you're still female."

"You're being way too premature."

"Perhaps." Her expression belied the word.

Later, driving home and thinking over the evening, Jo realized with dismay she hadn't yet thanked Grey for his actions during the accident. She doubted she could make him understand how much his calm presence had meant to her, but she owed him the words, nevertheless. She hadn't fallen asleep once since that day without thinking about how it would have been to lie trapped in the dark alone. She didn't that night, either.

Jo strolled through the mist of an unseasonably warm morning, the Sunday edition of *The Times-Picayune* under her arm, dodging the moisture that dripped from cast iron balconies overhead. Wet patches on the uneven sidewalk glistened dully in the tempered light and foghorn blasts from Algiers Bend punctuated the early quiet.

She inhaled deeply, savoring the mingled scents of the French Quarter — creosote and catfish, damp bricks and old plaster, spices from the restaurants already preparing for the noon meal, coffee brewing thousands of miles from its Brazilian origins. A horse-drawn carriage clip-clopped down the street carrying a tourist family bent on a sightseeing head start. She waited for it to pass, then crossed Decatur Street to her destination.

A saxophonist stood on the pavement outside the Cafe du Monde drawing bluesy notes from the instrument in his hands. She paused to drop a dollar into the open case at his feet. The musician nodded his thanks, never missing a beat in the open-air recital. Jo smiled, before ducking under the green and white striped awning and stepping into the coffee shop.

The aromas of fried dough and hot coffee hung temptingly in the warm interior as she made her way to her favorite corner. From her seat on the shabby vinyl chair she could see the river on one side and across the street on the other, the fat pigeons on the iron fence around Jackson Square. She gave her order for beignets and cafe au lait to a waitress and settled back to enjoy the paper.

She had worked her way through two cups of coffee, three sugar-dusted beignets, and the society column when his voice broke into her self-indulgence.

"Is this seat taken, or can anyone sit here?"

She looked up, already smiling in recognition. "Grey! What a nice coincidence."

"No coincidence. You mentioned last night you spent Sunday mornings here. I shifted my regular route hoping to catch you."

"Your route?"

"Running." He indicated the sweats and jogging shoes he wore.

"Of course. Please, sit down." She folded the paper she had been reading, clearing space on the table.

Grey signaled a waitress, giving her his order for coffee, before taking the chair across from Jo.

A ruddy glow from his run marked the planes of his cheekbones as he smiled. His zippered sweatjacket opened far enough to allow her a view of the strong column of his throat, where a pulse beat steadily beneath the tan skin. She could almost feel that pulse under her fingertips. The sensation surprised her.

She had to remind herself to talk. "Did you get your problem last night handled all right?"

She thought his smile lost some of its warmth. "Yes. I was sorry to have to leave early."

Apparently, he didn't intend to explain his reason for doing so.

"I've already called Vivian to make my apologies," he said and grimaced. "They might have carried more weight if I had remembered how much she likes to sleep in."

Jo laughed. "I don't think she'll hold it

against you. I got the impression you were her fair-haired child."

"Guilty as charged. Vivian spoiled all of us shamelessly when we were growing up. If I was in trouble at home, I could always count on Viv for sympathy and chocolate chip cookies."

"I imagine you went through a lot of cookies."

He grinned. "Dozens."

The waitress brought his coffee, and he paused. After she left, he wrapped his hands around the heavy ceramic mug and leaned forward, his forearms, exposed by the sleeves he had pushed up, resting on the table. "I hope it wasn't awkward for you after I left."

"In what way?" she said, keeping her expression carefully blank.

He directed a knowing glance at her. "Vivian is neither stupid nor insensitive," he said. "Even if she were both, she couldn't have failed to notice there's something between us. When she wants information, she can be tactfully subtle or ruthlessly direct. So . . . I'll ask again. Was it awkward?"

Talk about ruthlessly direct. "Actually, no. She was in her tactfully subtle mode. Most of the time," she added, remembering Vivian's later comments.

"Then you got off lightly. Good. Maybe it will make the conversation we're going to have now easier for you."

"I beg your pardon."

"There *is* something between us. Isn't there?"

She feigned a sudden interest in the snowfall of powdered sugar that dotted the table from the beignets, brushing it off with her fingertips.

"Isn't there, Jo?" he insisted, demanding she answer him.

Her lashes lifted, and she met his blue gaze. "Yes."

"So what are we going to do about it?" he questioned.

She shook her head slightly and waited. She was sure he would tell her.

"Nothing," he said.

She stared at Grey in surprise. That was not the answer she expected.

A corner of his mouth pulled into a smile. "There's no doubt in my mind over what I want" — his eyes heated momentarily — "but we're not going to do anything about it because you aren't sure yet. I won't push you into something you're not ready for. You're not ready, are you?" His hopeful tone of voice brought the smile to her face she knew he intended.

"No. I'm sorry."

"Don't apologize. You have a right to your feelings. Besides," his smile turned cocky, "I expect them to change soon." His wink teased a laugh from her.

"Thank you for understanding," she said.

He dropped the joking demeanor. "I hope you still feel that way in a few minutes. This is where the conversation starts to get hard." He glanced down at his mug, his expression thoughtful, then back up to her eyes. "Last night, when I kissed you. What was that?"

"I'm not sure I understand what you mean," Jo told him warily.

"All evening long you were sending signals that a kiss was the least of what you wanted from me. At least I thought you were. Was I wrong?"

Meeting his gaze was almost more than she could manage, but honesty compelled her to answer him. "No."

"Then what happened? You went from hot to cold in the space of a heartbeat."

"I, uh . . . not cold exactly."

"Then what . . . exactly?"

She stared over his shoulder, trying to find the words.

He pushed aside his coffee cup and reached to take her hands, clasped tightly together on the tabletop. "Honey, you told me about the rape. Is this really so much harder to talk about?" A crease deepened in his cheek. "Just pretend it's dark, we're cold, wet, and buried under several tons of rubble."

She gave him a fleeting smile at his gentle teasing, and looked at his hands holding hers warmly. Taking a deep breath, she prepared to explain what she wasn't sure she understood herself. "You were right. I did want you to kiss me." She refused to admit to more than that.

He watched her closely. "Okay . . ." He nodded, indicating for her to continue.

"I don't know what happens. It's like suddenly I feel nothing."

Grey frowned. "You're not talking about just us, are you?"

Her breath came out in a disheartened sigh. "No."

"Is it always like that for you?"

"Yes."

He was quiet for a moment, his thumbs rubbing absently over the back of her hands. "Jo, have you had sex since you were raped?"

She stiffened at the intimacy of the question, and tried to draw her hands away, but he held tight. Rather than engage in a juvenile tug-of-war, she relaxed and allowed them to remain in his hold.

"Grey, I'm twenty-nine years old," she said and hoped her exasperated expression would put an end to the conversation.

"I'm aware of that," he told her, unintimidated. "Just answer the question. Come on, dark, wet, cold, rubble, remember? Close your eyes if it helps."

She rolled them heavenward, instead, at his silly suggestion and told him grudgingly, "Yes, I've had sex."

His mouth quirked at her reaction. "How was it?"

"Like I just told you."

"You mean you just stop feeling?"

"Uh huh."

"Every time?"

She squirmed. "Yes, every time. Can we talk about something else now?"

"Not yet. Do you think it's because you're afraid?"

"I don't know. Maybe." She shrugged a shoulder. "Sometimes."

"Then why do you do it?"

"I guess I keep hoping it will be different. But it never is."

"When *I* kissed you, were you afraid of *me?*"

Her gaze flew to his. The one thing she could never be, was afraid of this man. She smiled and told him sincerely, "No."

He studied her face searchingly, as though testing for truth. Apparently, what he found satisfied him, because he smiled back gently. "Good. You don't need to be. Ever. If not afraid, then what?"

How could she tell him? "I wasn't afraid of *you*. I was afraid —" She stopped, closing her eyes briefly. "This is so hard, talking to you like this."

He squeezed her hands. "I know. But I want to understand. Tell me. You were afraid . . ."

She gnawed on her bottom lip for a moment. "It felt different with you. *I* felt different with you. Sexier. You know."

His mouth slanted in a wry smile. "Yeah. I do."

"Anyway, I was afraid that when you kissed me, the same thing would happen that always does, that suddenly the wonderful feeling would stop."

He appeared to think over her words, before the corners of his mouth quirked up. "But it didn't, did it?"

She tried, but couldn't prevent the tiny smile that tipped up the corners of her own mouth. "No."

His hands gave hers a last squeeze and released them. "Okay, question and answer period is all over with. You held up well. *Now* we can talk about something else." He lifted his mug and sipped, his eyes smiling over the rim.

She huffed out a breath of exasperated laughter. "I'm not sure what we could possibly talk about now that wouldn't sound ridiculously anticlimactic."

"How 'bout this. I want to take you out, spend some time getting to know you, have you get to know me. With the beginning we had, we got short-changed on the details. Let's back up and start over."

She tipped her head and regarded him. "That sounds good. I'd like that."

"Great. But there's something I want you to do for me first."

"What's that?"

"I'd like you to relax with me. I won't pressure you for anything. We're just going to take it easy and let whatever happens happen. I don't want you waiting for me to put moves on you. If there are any moves to be made, you'll have to be the one to make them. Agreed?"

She took a moment to marvel over the novelty of a relationship with no pressure, no demands, and couldn't help a generous dollop of skepticism. His expression betrayed only honest concern. He wasn't the kind to say something he didn't mean.

"Agreed."

"Good." He pushed back his chair and stood. "Let's go for a walk. Check out the progress they've made cleaning up Riverwalk."

As they strolled slowly along Decatur, Grey grasped Jo's hand casually, aware she tensed slightly. She would get used to being touched by him. He intended to do it often. Nothing threatening; just a hand at her waist, an arm around her shoulders, a handclasp.

He would teach her to welcome his touch, even crave it, teach her to trust her body's urging and capacity for pleasure. The promise in her eyes assured him of that.

He just hoped she didn't take too long doing it; hoped he could live up to his own promise — that he would put no pressure on her, let her come to him when she was ready. Already he found himself watching her mouth, wanting to take it in a kiss that was hard, hot, and deep, not the chaste exchange of the evening before. If he rushed her, she'd freeze. He could wait. The waiting might half-kill him, but he could wait.

Because of the investigation he should have been distancing himself from Jo. Instead he found himself more personally involved than ever. She drew him like no woman he'd known. Professionally he sought evidence, but personally he would have staked his tenure on her innocence.

They reached the barricades around the mall where reconstruction was already underway, and paused. The only sounds were the usual boat whistles, the chatter of pedestrians in a variety of languages, and the bells from Saint Louis Cathedral across the way. The shouts of construction workers yelling directions to one another were a far cry from the desperate calls for help that had tormented him earlier.

"Hard to believe, isn't it?" Jo said quietly.

He glanced down at her. "Just what I was thinking."

Her face turned up to his, her expression serious. "I never thanked you for your quick action that day, for doing what you could to protect me. I was paralyzed. I think if you hadn't been there, I'd have still been in the store when the ship hit."

Grey looked at the section of the mall where her shop used to be, marked only by the jagged ends of sheared steel girders, and suppressed a shudder. "You don't owe me any thanks. I did what I could to save myself. You just happened to be along."

"You covered my body with yours. From my point of view, that was a pretty heroic act."

He tipped a wry smile at her. "It wasn't by choice. Circumstances dictated the arrangement."

Her brows arched. "That's not the way I remember it."

"Then your memory is playing tricks. You must have gotten hit on the head, too."

His voice lost the teasing note. "I'll tell you what I remember. I remember a woman with a voice like warm honey who talked to me, who told me things she probably didn't want to to distract my attention from my pain. She gave me a piece of herself in an attempt to lighten my suffering. You want to talk about heroic — that's heroic."

His gaze held hers, daring her to dispute his words. "All right," she finally said, "I concede that we're both wonderful people. Let's drop it."

He chuckled and turned them to walk back in the direction they had come. "Where's your apartment?"

She told him and they strolled toward it, in no hurry. The sun had burned through the fog, blessing them with a beautiful day. Jo slowed as they walked past the damp, mottled wall of a building. In a city built below sea level, keeping the plaster intact was a full time job. It had fallen off in areas of the wall, exposing the brick beneath.

"Isn't that beautiful?" she breathed.

Grey cocked a brow. "I'm not sure that's the first word that would have come to mind for me."

"No, it is," Jo asserted. "Look at that mellowed texture. You can't buy that kind of patina. Only time can do that. One of the reasons I love the Quarter is that it's so old."

Grey stepped carefully around a broken section of sidewalk yet to be repaired. "I won't argue with that."

"I'll grant you the Quarter has its problems, but we're working on them. I think the signs of age are like character lines on a face — honestly come by through life experience, I wouldn't change a thing."

"Not even the bad plumbing?"

She laughed. "All right, you caught me. I guess I do get a little carried away."

"I'm just kidding you. Actually I've always been fond of the Quarter." They passed under the balcony of the Pontalba Apartments, the iron railings as ornate and delicate as Chantilly lace. "It's like a woman — voluptuous, secretive, bawdy, even wicked sometimes. Rather like an aging courtesan."

She looked up at him, tipping her head consideringly. "I like that description. Pretty romantic words for a professor."

"Aren't college professors allowed to be romantic?"

"None of the ones I ever had seemed to be."

"What was your major?" Grey asked.

"Business."

"There's your problem. Business professors have calculators for brains. Anthropology instructors on the other hand . . ." He wiggled his brows suggestively, drawing a laugh from Jo.

Jo paused before a heavy wooden gate painted a deep wine-rose. "This is my place." Her smile went from being relaxed and natural to a jerky tug at the corners of her mouth. "Would you like to come in for coffee or something?"

Grey's gaze took in the hand worrying her purse strap and decided to let her off the hook. He made a show of glancing at his watch. "I'd like to, but there are two hundred fifty final exams waiting to be graded. I want to get them finished before Christmas. Give me a raincheck?"

"Of course." He tried not to be insulted by the relief in her voice.

"Good. I'll see you for Christmas then at Vivian's."

"I'm looking forward to it." Her lips curved in a smile that appeared to come more easily.

Before she had a chance to worry again, Grey grasped her chin and tipped her face up. He pressed a kiss on her mouth, holding it only a few seconds, before straightening. "Me, too."

He turned and strode away quickly up the sidewalk before she could guess how affected he'd been when her lips had softened in sweet response.

Chapter Four

Vivian's glossy black front door swung open and Jo was greeted by a smiling Grey, looking very collegiate in dark slacks and a tweed sweater. He held a silver punch cup containing what appeared to be eggnog. "Come in, I've been waiting for you."

"Am I late? I'm sorry," Jo said, stepping inside.

"You're not late, I'm impatient." Grey closed the door behind her and eyed her long skirt and tapestry vest. A soft wool shawl around her arms in an ash-of-roses color completed the ensemble she knew set off her blond looks.

She gripped the packages she held tighter. "I hope this outfit is all right. I wasn't sure what the dress would be."

"It's beautiful. I was just thinking what perfect taste you have."

"I like *you*, don't I?" she asked lightly.

"I hope so." Grey's gaze warmed, his eyes signaling his intent. The fingers of his free hand cupped her cheek, and she found herself on the receiving end of a kiss that paralyzed her with its tenderness.

She stood stunned by the warmth of his mouth, the pleasure of his touch as his lips gently crushed hers. She wanted to reach for him, but the packages filled her arms. The quiet purr that hummed newly in her throat surprised her.

She caught his already familiar scent of woods and spice and clean male, and closed her eyes, savoring the flood of exquisite sensations. Much too soon it seemed, he lifted his mouth from hers. She blinked, feeling disoriented, and thought she detected a gleam of satisfaction in his gaze.

"Merry Christmas," he told her softly, and pointed to the gilded wire ball full of mistletoe hanging over her head. "I come from a long line of romantics."

She glanced up. "So it would seem. Merry Christmas yourself."

"Let me take those." He reached for the packages she held. "I hope you didn't feel obligated to bring something."

"I didn't feel obligated. I wanted to." For too many years she had been denied the luxury of gift-giving. She enjoyed finally being able to buy things for the people she cared about and indulged herself joyfully.

She hoped Grey would like the sweater.

She hadn't intended to give him such a personal gift, but one of the colors in its variegated pattern had echoed the blue of his eyes and she'd had to have it.

He balanced her gifts easily in one arm and pressed a hand to the back of her waist. "Come on in and meet the rest of the crew."

Vivian greeted her warmly while Grey placed her gifts under the tree. He straightened and introduced her to his older sister Andrea and her husband Paul Carpenter. Jo learned that Paul was a cardiologist. The two doctors had juggled their busy schedules to enable them to spend the day together with family. Andrea's dark fringe of bangs accented eyes that regarded Jo with friendly curiosity. Jo, normally reserved with new acquaintances, liked her instantly.

At his introduction, Grey's younger sister Sarah turned from the punchbowl on a sideboard and extended a cup. "Hi. Merry Christmas. Vivian's just been telling us about Grey's and your experience at Riverwalk. It must have been harrowing."

Jo accepted the eggnog and took a moment to study the strikingly beautiful face framed by dark, shoulder-length hair. Sarah's expression reflected genuine concern.

A glance at Grey leaning against the mantle showed her he waited as curiously as the others for her answer.

"It would have been more so without Grey there, but I won't embarrass him by recounting how wonderful he was."

He grinned. "Go ahead. Embarrass me."

Sarah pulled a face at him. "You always were such a show-off."

Conversation became general, moving from Jo's business to the Carpenters' hospital stories to the contract for decorating a new office building that Sarah had recently garnered. Vivian bounced back and forth from living room to kitchen, refusing all offers of help, insisting that her guests relax and get acquainted. When it was time to put the meal on the table, the younger women overrode her objections and carried the numerous dishes to the table. After places were sorted out and everyone was finally seated, Vivian asked Grey to say grace.

His quiet voice warmed Jo in a way that, given the circumstances, she suspected was improper. After saying grace, Grey raised his head and caught her gaze across the table, an answering warmth lighting his eyes. Vivian proposed a toast, and Jo reached gratefully for her wineglass.

"To Christmas," Vivian said, "and to friends and family with whom to share it."

The toast brought a lump to Jo's throat and she swallowed her wine with difficulty. The Christmas season was always a painful time for her. This year seemed harder than ever — maybe because her emotions felt scraped raw since the accident. Surrounded by Grey's family, seeing the love they obviously shared, she suddenly feared she would embarrass herself with tears. She saw Grey regarding her, a line between his brows, and made a hurried comment on the beauty of the table.

"Vivian, you must have been cooking for days."

"Yes, but you know how much I enjoy it. I'm not home long enough for it to feel like drudgery. Do try the artichokes. It's a new recipe, and I'm using you all for guinea pigs."

By the time they had worked their way to the mincemeat pie with whipped cream, Jo wasn't sure she could stand without groaning. Paul leaned back in his chair and patted his flat stomach. "Your experiment was a success and then some, Vivian. I am one satisfied guinea pig."

"Make that two," Grey echoed. "Let's have after dinner drinks in the living room.

Jo brought goodies and I've waited as long as I can to open mine."

"What makes you think one of those boxes is for you?" Jo asked.

"I peeked," he admitted, smiling shamelessly.

"Well you're just going to have to wait a little longer," Sarah told him. "You sit, Vivian, and let us clean up." Her comment was seconded by both Andrea and Jo.

"Gladly," Vivian agreed. "I'll enjoy having the men to myself for a while."

"No, you won't. They're going to help clean up, too. Come on, guys. Up and at 'em," Sarah ordered.

Grey stood and reached for plates. "That Napoleonic complex must be to make up for being the baby in the family," Grey said in a loud aside to Paul.

Sarah stuck her tongue out at Grey before disappearing into the kitchen. With the men shuttling leftovers and dishes, and the women dealing with them, clean-up was quickly handled. Soon everyone settled happily back in the living room.

"*Now* can I open my present?" Grey asked his younger sister with exaggerated civility.

Sarah nodded, as lofty as a queen granting favors.

"Jo?" Grey waited.

"Please," she said. "And pass out the others."

Grey's sisters and brother-in-law were clearly surprised at being on Jo's gift list. She assured them the gifts were only tokens to show her appreciation at being included in the family meal.

No one opened their gifts immediately, waiting instead to see what Jo had given Grey. He ripped off the paper as heedlessly as a child and lifted the box top. Pushing aside tissue paper, his hands pulled the sweater out. "How did you know blue was my favorite color?" he asked, pleased surprise evident in his voice.

"I didn't. It's mine." At least a certain shade of it. "I thought it would look good on you."

"At the risk of sounding immodest, I think it will, too." He held the sweater against his chest, checking the fit, then folded and replaced it in the box. "Thank you, Jo." His eyes promised her a more private thank-you later.

She met his gaze, smiling bravely. "You're entirely welcome."

Vivian opened her gift, and her happy exclamation drew Jo's attention from Grey. Jo had found an unusual antique cup and saucer for the collection Vivian maintained. "Thank you, Jo. You know I love it."

Vivian held the set carefully, turning it in her hand and examining it from all sides. Finally she rested the cup and saucer in her lap. "Grey, fetch Jo's gift from me from under the tree, would you?"

Beautiful paper covered the box and Jo took a moment to enjoy the elaborate bow and sprig of holly that decorated it. Her fingers carefully slid the ribbon off and set it aside. Anticipation of the gift was part of the experience and she lingered over the opening, drawing it out. After peeling away the tape, she removed the wrapping paper and folded it.

"Good Heavens, Jo. You make opening a present a ceremony," commented Sarah. "Certainly makes Grey's technique look crass."

Grey glared at his sister in mock displeasure. "I get the job done."

Jo ignored them and parted the layers of pink tissue paper veiling the gift. "Oh, Vivian, what have you done?" she murmured reverently.

Her fingers grasped the narrow straps of an ivory silk nightgown and lifted the confection from its box. Lace as gossamer as a sigh filled the front in a deep "V" that plunged below the waist. The silk that puddled in her lap was hardly heavier than moonbeams.

Vivian seemed pleased with her reaction. "It looked made for you. I know how much you love beautiful lingerie."

Jo felt Grey's gaze on her. His expression told her louder than words he visualized her in the provocative garment. A quick, not unpleasant frisson shivered through her at the thought of standing before Grey clothed in the silken haze.

"It's gorgeous, Vivian. Thank you so much."

"You're welcome, dear. Now put it to good use."

Jo's head came up in surprise, and at Grey's laugh, she cursed the flush that warmed her cheeks.

"Viv, you've embarrassed her," Grey said. "Behave yourself."

"I don't have to behave myself. I'm old."

Grey snorted. "Not old enough. Sometimes I feel more like your uncle than your nephew."

Jo was grateful for their bantering. It gave her the respite she needed. By the time Grey's sisters expressed their appreciation for the attractively bound journals, she had recovered her equanimity.

Paul thanked her for his gift of a set of golf balls. "How did you know I played?"

Jo planted her tongue in her cheek. "Isn't golf a required subject in medical school?" At the general snickers, she lost her innocent expression. "Actually, Vivian mentioned it once."

"Now for the *pièce de resistance*." Grey stood and rubbed his hands together, before walking to the tree where the one remaining present stood. It was an oddly-shaped bundle almost three feet high, wrapped in butcher paper. The only concession to Christmas was a large red bow stuck on the side. "My gift to Jo."

"You didn't need to get me anything," Jo protested.

"No," he agreed. "I didn't. I wanted to." He smiled at the echo of her earlier words. "You're not the only one allowed to buy presents."

When he bent and lifted the obviously heavy object, Jo's curiosity ratcheted up a notch. He carried it to her and set it on the floor in front of her, grunting slightly as he did so. She stared, mystified as to what it could possibly be.

"Grey wouldn't even give us a hint when he brought it in. We're all dying to know what it is," Andrea told her.

"Go ahead," Grey urged. "Open it."

She rose from her chair and knelt on the floor, reaching gingerly for an edge of paper. At the peek that was revealed, she became more mystified than ever. She ripped off the rest of the paper quickly and sat back stunned by what it had concealed.

No one spoke. Sarah and Andrea exchanged a look that said clearly they questioned either Grey's taste or his sanity. Even Vivian withheld comment.

All eyes focused on the filthy angel that stood before Jo, her weathered stone face holding an expression of quiet serenity. Water, lichen, mold, and God-only-knew-what-else had mottled her skirts and aged her wings, accenting every fold and feather. Dark streaks ran like tears down her cheeks, and a large chunk where the tip of one wing should have been had broken off in the distant past.

"Oh, Grey," Jo breathed softly. "She's wonderful."

Sarah and Andrea looked at Jo, amazement mirrored on their faces. "She is?" Sarah asked.

"Yes, she is," Jo assured her, her gaze still riveted by the statue. Finally she turned to Grey. "Where ever did you find her?"

He smiled lopsidedly. "You don't want to know."

Her gaze returned to the statue. No gift had ever meant as much to her as the time-gentled object before her. Grey had listened to her, had understood when she talked about her love for the French Quarter. His understanding was a greater gift than the angel. Already half in love with him, she felt herself tumble the rest of the way.

"I don't know how to thank you."

He smiled wickedly. "We'll think of something."

Shortly afterward, Andrea and Paul announced they needed to leave. They were driving back to Baton Rouge that night since Paul had rounds the next morning. They thanked Jo again and promised to be back when the new store opened. Sarah left right behind them, hinting she'd love to give Jo a hand with the design of the new shop.

When Vivian returned from seeing Sarah to the door, Jo stood. "I should probably be going, too. I took the day off today. I need to get back to work bright and early tomorrow."

"I'll follow you home and carry the angel in for you," Grey told her. "She's too heavy for you."

"I appreciate that, but are you sure it's

not too far out of your way?"

Vivian waved away Jo's concerns. "He wouldn't have offered if he hadn't meant it," Vivian assured her. "Besides, I feel better, knowing he'll be with you. The Quarter can be dangerous at night for a woman alone."

Grey carried the statue out to Jo's car while she made her thanks to Vivian for the evening. When she reached her car, he stood beside the open door and waited for her to get in. "She's in the trunk. I'll follow you home and then you can show me where to put her."

He shut the door and Jo watched in the rearview mirror as he jogged to his own car, a black Mustang convertible. She started her engine and waited until he drew up behind her, then moved off from the curb. Although she had never been nervous driving at night, looking up into the mirror and seeing his lights lent her a new reassurance.

In the Quarter, she turned into the alley behind her house and eased her car into the much-coveted parking space that came with it. Grey drew up behind her and motioned for her to stay put until he parked. A few minutes later she saw him stride quickly toward her from further up the street.

Jo stepped from her car and reached back to pick up her purse and the box containing the nightgown. After she opened the trunk, Grey bent and wrapped both arms around the statue while Jo unlocked her back gate. He heaved the angel out of the trunk and followed Jo into the brick-paved courtyard garden.

Grey looked around curiously. The lights Jo had left burning revealed a charming space, lush with potted plants even in winter. Ornamental cabbages contrasted colorfully against a variety of greenery. Topiary bushes trimmed in formal shapes gave the space the same European air he remembered from her store. Although the potted rose trees stood bare of leaves and blossoms, he could imagine their fragrant beauty come spring.

"This lady's getting heavy," Grey puffed. "Where do you want her?"

Jo dropped her purse and the box on a lacy, white iron table and quickly shifted pots, creating an open space in one corner. "Right here, for now."

He set the statue down where she indicated, and they both stepped back to survey the effect.

"She's perfect," Jo said. "She looks like she's been there forever." She turned her face up to his. "I love her, Grey. Thank you again."

He smiled down into her eyes and wondered if she'd remember his earlier teasing comment about finding a way to express her gratitude. He watched awareness blossom in her expression — watched her pupils dilate and her lips part. His gaze centered on her mouth for a moment as he considered the circumstances.

"You're expecting me to kiss you again, aren't you, Jo? Perhaps even hoping I will."

Her lashes dropped and her focus seemed to be somewhere in the middle of his chest. "Yes," she said, her voice so quiet he could hardly hear it.

"But you're afraid to invite it, because you're afraid I might misunderstand, might expect more than you think you're ready to give."

"Yes," she murmured again.

He put a finger under her chin and lifted it, wanting to see her eyes. "I told you before, I won't make a move you haven't asked for first. For now, we'll just try a kiss. Don't worry I'll push you farther. I won't."

Her gaze searched his, before her hand reached and tentatively cupped the back of his head. Her fingers exerted a slight pressure as she offered him her mouth.

He brushed her lips softly, then lifted enough to speak against them. "Be easy with it, honey. Enjoy the feeling. If it's good, go with it. Experiment. You're safe."

He waited a beat, and she encircled his neck with both arms, bringing his mouth back firmly to hers. She appeared to take him at his word. He prayed he could keep it. His hand slid from her chin to behind her jaw, his thumb at its feminine curve, his fingers spearing into her hair.

When her tongue slid timidly over his bottom lip, he almost groaned aloud. He returned the caress, and her mouth opened unhesitatingly. He slipped inside, careful not to take her too deep too fast. Her tongue touched his, and he let her taste him for a moment before he responded.

Jo pressed closer, but he knew the action was unconscious. He stroked his hand down her back, exerting great force of will to stop at her waist when he wanted to cup her bottom and pull her up tight against him.

When she opened her mouth wider under his, he took the hint and plunged his tongue deeper, tasting her more fully. She tilted her head, kissing him from a new angle, bringing them closer. At the tiny noises she began making, his fingers tightened at her waist, and he commanded himself to hold them there.

Her teeth nipped at his lip and he reached his limit. He lifted his head abruptly and used the hands at her waist to shift her from him. At the confusion on her face, his jaw flexed.

"I'm sorry, honey, but if we're going to keep this just a kiss — and we are — then we've got to stop now."

Her expression cleared and became contrite. "I wasn't even thinking of it from your side. I'm sorry, Grey."

He gave an abortive laugh. "For what? Becoming aroused? For God's sake, don't apologize for that. I'm not sure my ego could take it if you didn't. And don't apologize for not being willing to go farther. I wouldn't take you tonight if you begged me. When you decide you're ready to make love with me, I don't want the decision made in the heat of passion."

He dropped his hands from her waist and shoved them into the pockets of his slacks. "You have nothing to be sorry for."

"It doesn't seem fair to you."

"I'll live." He studied her face, her lips slightly swollen and still moist from their kiss, her eyes wide as she looked up at him earnestly. He slanted a wry smile at her. "I'm not saying it's easy, but you don't need to worry about me."

Jo pulled her shawl tighter around her shoulders. "Would you like to come in for a nightcap?"

"Thanks, honey, but *no one* is that strong, least of all me right now. We'll do it another time. Tell me, do you have plans for New Year's Eve?"

"I've been invited to a bash that friends are having, but my presence will hardly be noticed. I'd much rather spend the evening with you, if that's what you're inviting me to do."

"I am. The chancellor is hosting a small black tie affair. I'd like it if you'd go with me."

She smiled. "Done."

"Good. I'll pick you up at eight. Merry Christmas again."

He turned to go and the box lying on the table caught his eye. He thumped it with a knuckle. "Someday I'm going to see you in that. Count on it." He shot her a wink, before walking briskly from the courtyard.

Chapter Five

Over the next several days Jo wrestled with the decision to tell Grey about her background. She hoped it wouldn't matter to him, hoped he wasn't the kind of person who would let it matter. But her background mattered to her. Why shouldn't it matter to him?

It mattered that she didn't know her father, had no desire to know him. It mattered that her mother had been an embarrassment to Jo most of her life. Only recently had Jo gained the maturity to feel compassion for the woman who birthed her.

At Christmas she had felt like a fraud with Grey's family. They were all so close, so proud of one another. Growing up, Jo had resented the kind of children Grey and his sisters had been. Even now, she fought not to feel jealous of their vastly different childhoods.

She knew Grey cared for her. Look how amazingly patient he was being. But would he still care if he knew she didn't really belong in his social class; that for her, family was only a concept, not the fine lineage of upstanding citizens he could boast?

If he learned the truth about her parents would he regard her with faint disdain? Would he find polite excuses to no longer see her?

By the morning of New Year's Eve Jo had worried herself almost sick over the questions. She loved Grey. The experience was too new, too fragile to risk. She couldn't tell him. If he turned away from her, she would never recover. She couldn't keep the knowledge of her past from him forever, but surely it would be all right to pretend for just a little while longer that she was the woman he imagined her to be.

She dressed with care, wanting Grey to be proud of her with his colleagues. As she surveyed herself in the mirror, she found no fault with the cream colored evening suit she had chosen.

The slim skirt that skimmed the toes of her shoes made her appear taller and more slender than she was. The brocade jacket, with its wide satin cuffs and lapels, nipped in at her waist, accenting its curve. Her only accessory other than pearl earrings was the wine-red silk rose pinned to her lapel. Her matching lipstick threw her mouth into startling relief against her fair coloring. She had pulled her hair into a knot at the nape of her neck, but let a few tendrils frame her face, softening the effect.

She continued to stare at herself in the mirror, meeting her own gaze and challenging herself to be honest. Dressing, she had touched her pulse points with perfume, had stroked the crystal stopper between her breasts and over her thighs, not wanting to think too deeply about the reason she did so. It was time to 'fess up.

She had been dressing for a lover. That was the reason a satin and lace teddy lay silkily against her skin beneath the suit, why lace garters held up pale stockings as fine as cobwebs. For Grey. For his eyes.

But not just for Grey. The seductive woman-trappings were also a kind of armor in the battle she fought with herself. They gave her the nerve to try. Before the night was over, she planned to ask Grey to make love with her. New Year's Eve seemed an appropriate time to let old fears go, to welcome new joy into her life. If only her courage didn't fail her.

She picked up her small beaded purse from the bed and dropped her lipstick inside, checking that she had a comb, compact, money, identification, condoms. She hadn't hesitated over the last. She couldn't assume Grey would have some. If she succeeded in working up the nerve to ask for what she needed, she didn't want to be sabotaged by a lack of protection.

The buzzer outside her door rang and she hurried downstairs to answer it. She had left the gate off the latch so Grey could enter the courtyard, and she opened the door to him. The sight of him all in black, but for the starched pleats of his formal white shirt sent quick pleasure dancing down her spine. Even the satin cummerbund circling his lean waist was black.

His blue eyes regarded her with approval, his smile lazy, appraising, almost as though he suspected her plans. "You ready?"

She hoped so. She smiled through her trepidation and nodded, before stepping out and turning to lock her door. Grey escorted her to the Mustang, double-parked at the curb.

After they were underway, Grey reached across the gear shift and laid his hand on Jo's thigh. He felt her small flinch, but left his hand in place.

"You look beautiful tonight, Jo." She reminded him of a brandy alexander — all cool and creamy and sweet with a kick that took you by surprise.

"Thank you. You look very nice, too."

He glanced over, arching a brow. "My, aren't we proper tonight?"

His palm slid over her thigh, stopping when he encountered the hard, unexpected bump under her skirt. He traced the shape lightly with his fingertip and realized it was the fastener on a garter. "Or maybe not," he contradicted, throwing a speculative glance at her.

He removed his hand and down-shifted at a stoplight. "Some of that pretty lingerie Vivian said you liked?" He didn't really expect an answer. "After wondering all evening what you're wearing underneath, how am I supposed to keep my hands off you?" He worked hard for the teasing note as he accelerated again.

"I'm not sure I want you to," Jo answered.

His gaze cut to her. A car honked behind them, and he was forced to return his attention to the road. "You picked a hell of a time to tell me." He shoved the stick through the gears with more force than required.

"I don't know that I've told you anything. I just said I wasn't sure."

"Get back to me when you are." If the words came out a trifle grim, it couldn't be helped. A muscle in his jaw jumped, and he took a deep breath and blew it out slowly.

They made the remainder of the trip in silence, Jo's face turned away from him as she stared out the window. Grey cursed himself for his impatience, especially when he had promised her — and himself — otherwise.

He parked behind the row of cars already lining the curb in front of the chancellor's pseudo-French chateau in one of the new suburbs and walked around to open Jo's door. When he helped her from the car, her eyes held a question.

He squeezed her elbow. "Relax. It's okay, honey."

She smiled up at him with enough trust to shame a priest. "I know."

Inside, Grey introduced Jo to several other professors and their wives. Chancellor Kittrick welcomed her enthusiastically. "This one's a keeper, Grey."

Appropriating Jo's hand, Kittrick towed her off to meet his wife, leaving Grey staring after them wryly. Jo was in good hands for the moment. He'd rescue her in a few minutes. He went in search of the bar and a drink other than the champagne the circulating waiters had dispensed.

When he caught up to Jo again, Marie Stoddard, head of the drama department, was regaling her with stories from the previous year's Christmas party.

"Watch it, Marie. You're going to give her the wrong idea about us."

The buxom redhead chuckled richly. "Too late, sugar. I already have."

"And here I thought you academic types were stuffy." Jo's smile teased him from the corners of her eyes.

"Stuffy? Lady, it's obvious that a whole area of your education has been sadly neglected. We'll have to see what we can do about remedying that." He put his arm around Jo's waist. "Excuse us, Marie. There's no time like the present to get started."

He steered Jo toward the arched doorway at the other end of the room and felt a flash of annoyance at her hesitation.

"Grey?"

"Dance, Jo. We're just going to dance."

"Oh. Of course. I knew that."

The polished wood floor of the formal dining room, cleared now of furniture, gleamed under the chandelier's soft lighting. Several other couples were dancing to the small combo playing in one corner. Grey turned Jo into his arms and took her hand, moving them smoothly into the rhythm of the song.

For the first few minutes he simply enjoyed the sensation of holding her, letting his senses fill with her. He breathed in her spring-flower scent, sensual and sweet, and remembered the sound of her voice blocking out his pain the day of the accident. She felt small and feminine, but he knew from experience the depth of her inner strength. He liked the way her head came to just the right height to tuck under his chin if he were to pull her closer.

She danced easily with him, as though they had practiced for years. At the subtle directions of hand pressure or a nudge of his thigh, her body responded instantly, obeying his lead. He tried not to let himself wonder if she'd be the same way in bed.

"Grey?"

"Hmm?"

"How old are you?"

It took him a moment to drag his thoughts back to the dance floor. Looking down at her in puzzlement, he answered, "Thirty-four. Why?"

"It just suddenly occurred to me that I didn't know. In fact, there's a lot about you I don't know."

True enough. And until Customs wrapped up their current investigation, he intended to keep it that way. Wariness sharpened his focus. "Such as?"

"Why anthropology?"

He smiled in relief at the easy question. "My family has always loved to travel. Every school vacation we took off for some exotic point. I became interested in the similarities and differences between cultures. By the time I got to college my major was a foregone conclusion."

The song ended and the dancers applauded politely. Grey grasped Jo's hand to keep her from walking from the floor. She had relaxed as they danced. Another round wouldn't hurt. The combo began another selection, and she came to him again.

"But why teach?" she asked, picking up their conversation. "Shouldn't you be off studying primitive villages or digging up ancient ruins?"

"I've done both of those."

Her gaze surveyed his tuxedo jacket. "It's hard to picture you in dusty khaki." A mischievous smile tipped the corners of her mouth up. "Do you look like Indiana Jones?"

He smiled. "Yeah. I look exactly like Indiana Jones when I'm in the field."

She closed her eyes. "Oh, be still my heart."

He leaned his head down to murmur in her ear. "I've even got the whip."

Her eyes sprang open. "Really?"

At the shock on her face, he gave a laugh. "No, but I couldn't resist the opening. And I didn't miss that little leap that your pulse rate took, either, when I mentioned it."

"It did not."

His grin became wider. "Did, too."

A blush suffused her cheeks and she dropped her forehead on his shoulder with a groan. He brought their joined hands to her chin and tipped her face back up to study it. "Cute."

She rolled her eyes. "Me or my Technicolor complexion?"

"Both. I've always been a sucker for maidenly blushes. I'll have to make a point of wearing my Indy garb for you. I never realized what a turn-on it could be."

"Considering how irresistible you apparently are in that costume, why aren't you still digging potsherds instead of lecturing in a classroom?"

A momentary twinge dampened his pleasure. Was her familiarity with potsherds the result of broad reading or involvement with ancient finds? Surely an antique dealer would legitimately be acquainted with the word. He shrugged off his unease. The case was beginning to make him paranoid.

"You'd be surprised how quickly the novelty of living in a tent can wear off. And I get a great deal of satisfaction out of teaching students who are not even aware they need to learn."

"You mentioned that before. You must enjoy young people."

"I do. Very much."

"I'm not around them often. Most of the kids I see are the ones that mothers bring into the shop with them." She laughed. "An antique store does not bring out the best in a child."

"My mother would sympathize with you. She confiscated my GI Joe on a regular basis. The Louis XVI dining room table was such a great surface to drive his tank over."

Jo winced. "You didn't."

"Yeah, I did."

"Your mother was more than merciful."

"No doubt about it, the woman is going to love you." He didn't usually introduce the women in his life to his parents, but then Jo was unlike his usual women. A red flag went up at the thought, until he decided their dramatic beginning accounted for his peculiar feelings.

The song ended and the musicians announced they were taking a short break. Jo declared a desire to sample some of the delicious-looking food arrayed on side tables in the other rooms.

They circulated through the party, chatting with other guests. Sometimes Jo was on his arm, but other times they became separated. Grey always knew where she was, who she spoke with. He tossed a cheese cube into his mouth and washed it down with a sip of martini, before turning to the room. Almost as though he possessed radar, his gaze locked instantly on Jo speaking with Marge Kittrick, tall and slim like her husband and clothed in a long white dress.

Suddenly, a boy no older than two darted between guests and ran to the two women, wrapping his arms around Jo's legs. Obviously delighted with himself, the child laughed and tipped his head back. The smile froze on his face and his eyes went wide. Grey realized the boy had meant to grab his mother, but because of the similarity of Jo's skirt had mistakenly attached himself to her.

Before the child could give in to tears, Jo stooped and scooped him up, hefting him up to her hip. He regarded her warily, but was won over when Jo chucked him under his chin and offered him a cracker off the table beside her.

Grey approached the group and smiled. "He's growing up fast, Marge. Aren't you, Buddy?" He grinned at the boy, a favorite among the faculty. Although he had been a surprise, late-in-life baby, his parents cherished him, and he had become something of an unofficial mascot.

"I'll say," Marge agreed. "And a demon in the process. How did you get away from Amanda, Buddy?" she asked, referring to their teenage daughter. "If he were older, I'd expect to find her tied and gagged somewhere. Here, Jo, let me take him. I know he's heavy."

"No, no, he's fine. I don't get the treat of holding a young man as fine as this one very often." She and the boy smiled happily at each other, Jo either oblivious or uncaring of the crumbs he distributed liberally over her suit jacket.

Grey liked children, would have enjoyed having them, but he was unwilling to marry again just for the experience of kids. Whatever joys came with parenthood, they could in no way offset the misery he remembered from his venture into matrimony.

Buddy fingered the silk rose pinned on Jo's lapel. "Isn't it pretty?" she said. She smiled at the child, and Grey was struck by the yearning in her eyes.

"Pretty," the boy echoed, and grinned up at her.

"I think so, too, Buddy," Grey said. "You got a good eye."

Amanda, the Kittrick's fifteen-year-old, jeans-clad daughter arrived at the group breathless. "There you are, Buddy. I'm sorry, Mom. He snuck off while I was in the bathroom."

"That's all right, sweetheart. Believe me, I understand."

"Hello, Professor Cantrell. It's nice to see you again," Amanda told Grey.

"Hi, Mandy. How's my best girl?"

She nailed her younger brother with a look. "At the moment, annoyed. I'm sorry he bothered you," she said to Jo.

Jo smiled at the girl. "Not a problem."

"Mandy," Grey said, "this is Jo Flaherty, a friend of mine."

"It's nice to meet you, Ms. Flaherty. Let me take him off your hands now." Amanda reached and lifted the toddler from her, unaware of the regretful expression that filled Jo's eyes. "Say bye-bye, Buddy."

"Bye-bye," Buddy repeated dutifully and smiled again, showing off his baby teeth, before waving over Amanda's shoulder at them as she carried him from the room.

Jo watched until they were out of sight. "What charming children you have, Mrs. Kittrick."

"Thank you. We're passingly fond of them ourselves. And please, call me Marge. Buddy makes me feel old *enough* sometimes."

"Marge it is then," Jo said. "It's a lovely party. All the food is wonderful."

"Please help yourself to more. You'll have to excuse me. It's time for me to play the chancellor's wife again." She made a droll face, before moving off to fulfill hostess duties.

Grey's hand brushed lightly over the front of Jo's jacket, fingers itching to linger at the soft fullness of her breasts.

She turned a surprised face to him. "I beg your pardon."

He suppressed a grin at her ladylike outrage. "Crumbs. Buddy's technique needs a little polishing yet."

She glanced down, batting his hand away. "I can do it myself."

"Pity."

She flicked the last of the cracker crumbs out of the petals of the rose, before straightening for his inspection. "Okay now?"

His gaze traveled over her slowly, before finally settling on her face. "The censored version? You look gorgeous." He held her gaze for a moment, watched her eyes darken. The only thing that prevented him from taking her in his arms was the room full of guests. Guests that watched him curiously.

"Come on. There are some other people I'd like you to meet." With a hand under her elbow, he guided her to a small group.

An hour later Grey muttered to her out of the side of his mouth, "Are you as sick of talking about the accident as I am?"

"That depends. Are you afraid you'll run screaming into the night if one more person comments on how terrible it must have been?"

"No. I'm more afraid I might commit grievous bodily harm."

"There is one thing telling about it over and over has done, though. In a weird kind of way, it seems to have neutralized the horror of the experience. I'm even getting bored with it."

Before Grey could comment, Elizabeth Garret, physics professor, approached, short silver hair in striking contrast to her black-sequined dress. "Grey, do introduce me to your date. Bob Schwartz just told me the two of you were in Riverwalk when that freighter hit. It must have been terrible."

Grey glanced at Jo and knew he made a mistake. She struggled to maintain a straight face. Watching her mouth lose its battle against the smile that pulled at the corners was all the trigger he needed to lose his own control. His laugh burst out and Jo's followed suit. She clapped a hand over her mouth, but it didn't help.

Elizabeth's eyes narrowed as she looked from one to the other. "I should have known Bob was pulling my leg. How could I have been so gullible? Wait 'til I tell that jerk what I think of his latest stunt." Elizabeth spun on her heel, marching off in search of the hapless Bob.

Tears leaked from the corners of Jo's eyes, and she leaned into him, muffling her laughs against his chest. He threw an arm around her and tried to bring his own mirth under control. Finally Jo straightened away from him wiping a finger under her eyes and sniffling.

"Oh, dear," she said, a laugh still lurking in her voice. "I hope we haven't created a problem for you. I just couldn't help myself."

"Don't worry about it. I'll explain it to Liz next week. In the meantime, I think we could both use a drink." He shot his cuff and glanced at his watch. "Besides, it's almost midnight. Can't toast the New Year without champagne." He looked around for a waiter, but none were nearby. "I'll be right back. Don't go anywhere."

Jo watched him stride purposefully across the room and pressed a hand to the butterflies in her stomach. She had sworn to herself she would make a decision by midnight. She understood Cinderella's dilemma. Would the wonderful spell be broken then? But how long could she and Grey continue the way they had been? She vacillated, even as he approached carrying two glasses of champagne.

"Here you go. And just in the nick of time." He handed one of the glasses to her as Chancellor Kittrick began counting down the seconds.

"— Seven, six, five, four, three, two, one. Happy New Year everyone!" The combo broke into a mellow version of "Auld Lang Syne" while some of the more boisterous of the crowd rang noisemakers and tossed paper streamers.

"Happy New Year, Jo," Grey said softly.

She looked up at him and feared she

would melt in the warmth of his gaze. He dipped his head and pressed a kiss against her mouth, and the fear became a certainty. When he would have drawn away, she clung to him, lifting her face to maintain contact. He responded instantly, holding her close and bringing his mouth firmly against hers once again.

She opened her lips and Grey's tongue slipped inside to mate with her own. She had only a moment to thrill to the intimacy before Grey broke off the kiss and straightened, his eyes blazing down at her like blue flames.

She licked her lip, the taste of his mouth on hers yet. "Happy New Year, Grey." The decision was not so hard after all.

"It's certainly starting off that way." He clinked his glass against the one she had forgotten she held and took a healthy mouthful.

She sipped her own champagne and wondered how to best bring the subject up.

"Are you ready to leave?" Grey asked. "We don't have to stay any longer. I've made my appearance, talked to all the right people, and stroked the appropriate egos. Now I'd like to have you to myself for a while. You owe me a rain check. Want to pay up?"

"So-o-o romantic." She fluttered her lashes at him. "I declare, you just sweep a girl right off her feet."

Grinning, he slung an arm around her shoulder and nipped at her ear, sending her heart into arrhythmia. "That's the idea. Come on. Let's get out of here."

Chapter Six

Jo unlocked her front door and shoved it wide, inviting Grey to enter. She led him past the stairway just inside to her jewel box of a living room. Although it was small, she loved her home and had furnished it carefully.

She walked to the Louis XV salon table and turned on the French lamp. Light glowed softly through the smocked silk shade, illuminating the space with a rosy glow. She watched Grey stroll around the room, pausing to run a finger over the bronze bust on a table, perusing the books in the built-in bookcases.

At the fireplace he bent to smell the pink, out-of-season lilies on the mantel perfuming the air sweetly, before turning. "Your home is beautiful, Jo."

She dropped her purse on the chocolate-brown velvet sofa. "Thank you."

"Do you mind if I get a little more comfortable?" Without waiting for an answer, he tugged the ends of his bow tie, undoing it, and let them hang loosely, then unbuttoned the top button of his shirt. He rubbed the skin on his neck under the starched collar. "Much better."

"Please, sit down." Jo motioned to one of the nineteenth-century needlepointed chairs that flanked the fireplace.

Grey arched an eyebrow at the chair, as though questioning its ability to hold him, before settling into it. He stretched his long legs out before him, ankles crossed, and pushed the sides of his jacket open to shove his fists into his pockets.

Jo clasped her hands together nervously and rested them on the back of the sofa. "Would you like a cup of coffee or maybe a brandy?"

Grey's eyes studied her with lazy thoroughness. Enduring his silent scrutiny tightened her already-taut nerves even further. "Is that really what I'm here for, Jo?" he finally asked. "Coffee? Did you wear that pretty underwear just to serve me coffee? I know I invited myself, but you didn't have to let me in. Why did you?"

She returned his look and the hesitation left her. She took a deep breath and gathered her courage. "You're right. You're not here for coffee."

His indolent pose didn't change as his gaze continued to hold hers. "What then, Jo? You're going to have to spell it out for me. I need to know you're sure in your own mind what you want."

She grasped the edge of the sofa, wondering if she'd be able to stand if it weren't there. "I want you to make love to me."

There, it was out. Now let him deal with it.

His mouth softened into a smile. "Come here, honey."

On legs shaky with excitement, she went to him. He sat up and spread his knees, pulling her between them. She laid her hands on his shoulders and waited.

"When did you decide this?" he asked.

She looked down into his face and frowned. "Do you or don't you want to make love to me, Grey?"

His smile warmed. "What I want has never been in question. It's you I'm trying to be sure of. What I don't want is for this to be a spur-of-the-moment, champagne-induced decision that seemed like a good idea when the band was playing 'Auld Lang Syne.'"

The shakes left her abruptly. "Don't insult my intelligence." She released his shoulders and would have spun away from him, but his hands held firm on her hips.

"I am *not* insulting your intelligence, dammit. I thought I was being sensitive. We can do it the other way, if that's what you would prefer."

He hauled her down to sit on his knee, before grasping her jaw and planting a hard kiss on her mouth. A thrill shot through Jo straight to her core. She wrapped both arms around his neck and kissed him back just as fiercely.

He lifted his head and stared. At the confused surprise in his expression, amusement tempered her passion. "At last. I thought you were going to talk all night."

His eyes lit. "Not when there are better things to do," he murmured and lowered his mouth in a kiss that was slower, gentler than the first.

Jo felt her bones go soft and relaxed against him. His tongue slipped between her lips and she met him with her own. He slid an arm under her knees and stood, cradling her against him, still holding the kiss. Jo's breath was coming in pants by the time he broke it off.

He glanced at the couch and shook his head. "Too short. Where?"

She snuggled closer and kissed his neck. "Up the stairs."

He shifted her higher in his arms and started for them.

"Wait," Jo told him. "I need my purse."

"Why?"

"Condoms."

"Now who's being insulting? What kind of Prince Charming would I be if I made the fair lady provide her own protection? Don't worry about it. Now, where were we? Oh, yes. On our way to bed."

At the bottom of the stairs Jo lifted her head from his shoulder. "You'll have to put me down," she said, her voice tinged with regret. "I appreciate the gesture, but we'll never make it up this way."

He eyed the narrow stairway. "I'm afraid you're right." He set her on her feet, keeping her close. "Let the record show that I made the effort."

"Duly noted." She smiled and reached for a kiss, before taking his hand and starting up.

At the top Grey followed her down a hallway past doorways to the master bedroom. A small bedside lamp glowed hardly brighter than candlelight. His quick glance took in the antique armoire with a beveled oval mirror on the front, the crystal chandelier, the intricately carved mahogany four-poster bed, before coming to rest on Jo's face.

In the soft light her eyes looked huge and dark as they gazed at him. He hesitated. Her spurt of self-confidence seemed to have deserted her. His hands came up and held her face, thumbs stroking over her cheekbones, lips.

"Cold feet?" he asked. "It's still all right to change your mind, you know."

"No. I won't back out."

"Flattering," he muttered dryly.

Deciding it was time to help her along, he covered her mouth in a kiss that demanded response. When she gave it to him in a quick gasp and parted lips, he pulled her closer, sliding his hands down her back.

He didn't stop at her waist, but let his hands smooth further down over the curve of her bottom. He waited for any sign of nerves, any slight tensing, but found none. The woman in his arms was as warm, as pliant, as giving as any he had ever held.

He pressed her to him, liked the way her pelvis tipped in answer. Her tongue flicked over his lip and he took the hint, sampling hers in turn. He waited for her invitation before taking her deeper. Tonight was Jo's night. He had gotten them started. Everything clsc was up to her.

He lifted his head, looked with satisfaction into her already heavy-lidded eyes. "Jo, I want you to do something for me."

"If I can."

"If at any time tonight things get scary

for you, I want you to tell me and we'll stop." He prayed she wouldn't ask, prayed he'd have the control to stop if she did. "Okay?"

"Okay. Now you do something for me."

"Anything."

"Take off your jacket. You're wearing way too many clothes."

His brow arched in surprise, before he complied and tossed the garment over a nearby chair. "Anything else?"

She tipped her head and considered him through her lashes. "Maybe your shirt?"

"Why Miz Flaherty, you shock me." He unfastened the cummerbund and dropped it with his jacket, then braced his hands on his hips. "You do it," he challenged with a grin, and waited.

Her lips twitched. "All right." She slipped her fingers into the neckline of the shirt and worked the first gold stud loose. She handed it to him and he slid it into his pocket. The second one proved more difficult, and her knuckles brushed lightly against his chest in her attempts to remove the fastener. It finally came free and Grey took it from her with relief.

By the time she had the third stud out, Grey found that maintaining his teasing smile required heroic effort. He quickly removed the cuff links from the sleeves and yanked the shirt tail from his trousers.

Jo had paused and stood uncertainly. "Going to chicken out on me now?" Grey taunted.

Her chin came up and she met his smile with a knowing one of her own. "Certainly not."

She placed her hands inside the shirt and flattened her palms on his chest. They felt cool, but hardly soothing, against his heated skin. She pushed the sides of the shirt open and skimmed her hands over his shoulders, peeling the shirt off. Her gaze never left his, and the mischievous gleam in her eyes told him clearly she knew the effect she was having.

"Enjoy the power, Jo," he warned. "This may be the last time I let you get away with it."

She tossed the shirt with his jacket. "Are you threatening me?"

"Better believe it." He grabbed her waist and pulled her close. "Maybe you ought to do something to stay on my good side."

"Like?"

"Use your imagination."

"W-e-l-l . . . how about this?" She encircled his neck and drew his head down, opening her mouth under his.

His tongue entered to stroke hers, touch behind her teeth, slide along the sensitive inner edges of her lips. She moaned and arched against him. He pulled her in tight, nestling his erection at the juncture of her thighs, then paused. If she were going to freeze, surely it would be now. She only held tighter and tipped her head at a new angle, taking the kiss deeper.

His mouth slid off hers to sample the delicate skin under her jaw. Although her present hairstyle gave him easy access to the whorls of her ear, he preferred its golden length loose.

He straightened and brought his hands to the sophisticated knot. "This has got to come down."

His fingers sought out and removed the pins, dropping them negligently on the dresser, before spearing into her hair and spreading the flaxen strands over her shoulders. "Much better. I've been wanting to muss up that ladylike appearance all evening."

His fingers played in her hair, massaged the back of her neck. Her eyes closed and she leaned her head back into his hands with a sigh. "That feels so good," she murmured.

A corner of his mouth lifted. "That's the idea."

His thumbs slid over her throat and traced her collarbones, while he marveled at the delicate softness of her skin. She tipped her head and purred at the light caress. His thumbs moved lower to follow the vee of her jacket neckline and she held her breath.

He repeated the action, lazily sliding up to her throat and then back over the beginning swell of her breasts as though there was nothing else he had in mind for the evening but absent-mindedly studying her neckline. By the fourth pass Jo's breathing had quickened nicely. He replaced his thumbs with a fingertip and let it dip lightly into her cleavage, feeling the press of her soft breasts, before withdrawing.

"Grey?"

"Hmm?"

She opened her eyes to gaze at him languidly. "Aren't you going to . . . ?"

"Are you rushing me, Jo?" Amusement colored his voice.

"No, I just . . ."

"Tell me. Anything you want, Jo, but I told you before, you'd have to ask."

"All right, damn you, touch me."

He chuckled. "Gladly. Like this?" He dipped his head and kissed her, while a hand stroked down her front to cup a gently-rounded breast. She returned his kiss urgently and breathed a quiet moan.

"I'll take that as a yes," he murmured, thumbing the nipple he could feel erect even through her clothes.

She pressed closer, arched higher, inviting him to take more. He caressed her other breast in the same way, closing his eyes on the sensations that touching her aroused in him. He fought the urge to hurry. Her breath rasped hotly as she squirmed against him.

"More, Jo? You know the rule. Ask."

Her lashes lifted and she directed an entreating gaze at him. "Please, Grey. Don't make me put it into words."

"Just for tonight, honey. You don't ever have to do it again, but tonight I want you to know you're in complete control of the show. Nothing happens without your say so."

She closed her eyes, took a heaving breath, and opened them again. "I want you to take off my jacket."

He pressed a soft kiss against her lips. "That a girl," he whispered, before moving to do as she asked.

He slid the garment down her arms and tossed it aside, then paused to regard her warmly. The white satin that only half-covered her breasts gleamed over the curves, and the tight peaks of her nipples stood out clearly beneath the luxurious fabric.

His fingers trailed over the tops of her breasts, before his hands moved to palm their heaviness gently. He felt her gasp and go still.

"Skirt, too, Jo?"

Her breath shuddered out. "Yes."

He reached around behind her and unbuttoned it, then eased the zipper down. He let the skirt puddle at her feet and held her waist while she stepped out of her shoes and skirt together.

His gaze traveled slowly up her legs encased in mist-sheer stockings, to the bare skin of her thighs exposed temptingly at the top. "God, Jo, you're even better than I've been imagining all evening."

He gave in to the temptation and ran his hands over her hips to the thighs that seemed more erotic for the contrast with the stockings. Jo moaned and reached for him, but he dropped to one knee, and her hands fluttered to his shoulders instead.

Following the path his gaze had just taken, he bracketed one delicate ankle and smoothed up her leg, the fine nylon slick under his palms. The warm flesh at the top had him lingering, stroking slower. He repeated his actions on her other leg and felt her quiver when his fingers brushed the damp heat between her thighs. He leaned forward and kissed the mound of her pubic bone through the satin.

Jo's fingers flexed on his shoulders. "Grey," she breathed, "I don't think I can stand up much longer."

Thank God. He stood and swept her up, then carried her to the bed and laid her on the white damask cover. He reached into his pocket and extracted several foil packets that he dropped on the nightstand.

Jo saw them and her eyes widened. "I thought you were Prince Charming, not Superman."

He smiled, enjoying the sight of her stretched across the bed, her long hair spread out around her face. "I believe in thinking positive."

He kicked off his shoes and quickly shucked his trousers, but left his briefs on. She'd feel more comfortable for the moment that way. He came down beside her, liking the way her arms reached to encircle his neck.

He kissed her, long and deeply, giving his passion more rein now that she was loosening up. She returned the kiss and arched under him, obviously wanting more. His hand glided over the satin covering her breast, fingertips bumping over the nipple and she arched higher with a whimper.

"Tell me, Jo." He was going hoarse.

Instead she pushed down one of the straps of the teddy, exposing a breast to his view and grabbed his hand. His heart lurched when she pressed his palm to the swollen nipple. He caressed the breast under his hand, rubbing the tip with his palm, circling the sweet weight with his fingers, pinching the nipple lightly between thumb and forefinger. Her moans and sighs told him more clearly than words she had forgotten to be afraid.

He sat up and eased the teddy down to her waist, giving him access to both her breasts. He began to give the second one the same treatment as the first, but she pushed his hand away and pulled his head down. "Please, Grey. Use your mouth."

He didn't need any more urging. He took a nipple between his lips and flicked it with his tongue, then felt it tighten further. He drew it into his mouth and sucked, and Jo cried out. He lavished both breasts with attention, alternately caressing the nipples lightly and suckling hard, pressing them against his teeth.

Jo's fingers fisted in his hair as she rocked against him.

"What else, Jo? What else do you want? Do you want me to take this off you? Touch more of you?"

"Yes, yes, please."

He knelt to unfasten her stockings, and his hand brushed the inside of her thigh as he released the garter. He could feel with his knuckle how wet the satin between her legs had become. Seeming accidentally to repeatedly brush against the damp, sensitive area, he took his time unfastening the second garter. Her thighs quivered and he thought the slightest press of his hand would have had her parting her legs wider for him.

He let her wait, unrolling the frivolous bits of nylon from her legs, before urging her hips up so he could pull the teddy off. Feeling her gaze on him, he looked up and found her eyes watching him, their expression ambiguous.

"Scared?" Please, no.

She shook her head. "More like impatient." She drew a deep, shaky breath. "For the first time I'm not in a hurry to get it over with. Just in a hurry."

He gave a quick laugh, surprised he was still able to. "All in good time. We'll get there."

He stretched out beside her and leaned over, assuring her of the truth of his words with a kiss that plundered her mouth erotically. His hand stroked down her body freely, the obstacle of clothing gone, before settling on the taut flesh of her pelvis, fingers splayed into the pale curls at its base. Her hips arched under his touch and a small mew issued from her throat.

He let two fingers slip further, easing them between the thighs that had gone lax. "Here, Jo? Is this where you want me to touch you?" He withdrew his fingers, teasing her with their closeness.

"Yes." Her answer bordered on a sob and she rocked higher against his hand.

He relented and touched her again, sliding his fingers between her folds to find her wet and ready for him. Each stroke of his fingers wrung a moan from Jo. He had never been with a woman as responsive as she was. Her eyes hadn't lied. He had known the passion was there.

When he slipped a finger inside her, she cried out softly. He drew it out slowly and then inserted two fingers and she whimpered, her fingernails digging deeply into his shoulders. He repeated his actions, feeling her arch higher against his hand with each probing caress. Her head tossed restlessly and he could feel the pattern of scratches her nails made on his back.

"Please, Grey. I can't wait any longer. Please take me."

He stripped off his briefs and grabbed one of the packets on the nightstand. After quickly rolling on the condom, he turned back to Jo. She lay ready for him, cheeks flushed, eyes wanting, thighs open to him. He could come just looking at her.

He moved over her, clasping her hands as he did so. He pinned them to the mattress on either side of her head, his fingers lacing with hers. His back already stung from her nails. He hated to imagine what it would feel like when they were done. The thought suddenly occurred that she might flash on the old memory of being held down, and he released her hands grimly.

He positioned himself between her legs and she reached her arms around his neck and tipped her hips up eagerly, before closing her eyes tightly.

"Open your eyes, Jo. Look at me." He didn't want her imagining being any other place with any other person than right there with him. Holding her gaze, he thrust in smoothly, burying himself with a groan deeply in her heat. He held perfectly still, regaining control and reining in his need for immediate release.

Jo lifted her legs and wrapped them around his waist, taking him even deeper inside. He hoped he wouldn't die before she climaxed.

He withdrew slowly, hearing her cry of protest, before he thrust back in. He did it a second time, then again, and yet again. At first he made an effort to be gentle, but finally driven by Jo's answering lunges, his only thoughts centered on the spiraling sensations driving him to completion.

Jo bowed tautly with a cry and he felt her convulse around him. Her sobs of fulfillment tipped him over the edge and his own release came quickly.

She had known it would be different with Grey. She just hadn't realized how much. He lay over her, breath still heaving in and out of his lungs, his head on the pillow beside hers. She turned her lips to his ear.

"Thank you, Grey," she whispered.

Amusement rumbled in his chest. "My pleasure."

"I'm serious."

He raised himself on his forearms and looked down into her face. "I know you are, but you don't owe me any thanks, honey. The capacity for pleasure was always there. You just finally felt safe enough for it."

"If I did, it's because of you. Because you made me feel safe. And loved."

Although he still held her, she would have sworn he distanced himself. He didn't love her. The disappointment hurt, but she could stand it. Few people in her life had loved her, but she had survived. Perhaps it would be enough that she loved him.

"Anyway," she said lightly, wanting to bring the warmth back into his eyes, "I'll thank you if I want to. That was the most fantastic, mind-blowing experience of my life."

"In that case, I take all the credit."

"I remember Sarah mentioned what a show-off you were."

"Honey, you ain't seen nothin' yet. Just give me a few minutes and I'll start to show you why I brought so many condoms."

She laughed, relieved to have made it through the awkward moment.

She woke to sunlight and memories. Grey had made love to her twice more and each time had been more intense than the one before. He had driven her higher than she ever thought possible. Freeing her from the fear that always blocked her pleasure was the most loving thing anyone had ever done for her. He might not love her, but he couldn't have been more tender if he did.

She stretched and smiled at the new aches the action produced. Perhaps more of what caused them would loosen them up. She turned, hand already reaching out to touch Grey.

His side of the bed was empty. Jo felt disconcerted for a moment until she reasoned he was probably in the bathroom. She snuggled into his pillow, savoring his fragrance still on it, and waited for him to return.

After what felt like several minutes, she blinked her eyes open. A perplexed frown creased her forehead and she lay still, listening for Grey. The only sounds that met her ear were the usual offerings of the Quarter.

Her gaze fell on the chair where he had tossed his clothes. Her own had been picked up and lay loosely folded, but Grey's were gone. She swallowed against the sudden nausea.

Her mention of love had spooked him. Why else would he have left her already? She was surprised at the way he had done it, though — just disappearing without a word to her. It struck her as cowardly, something she wouldn't have suspected of him.

The hurt cut too deeply for anger. How could he have made love to her with such patience, such understanding just a few short hours ago and then leave like she had been a one-night stand? He had all but turned her inside out. Remembering her response to him shamed her in the light of his cavalier attitude.

She felt hollow, too empty even for tears. She sat up and swung her legs wearily out of bed. The twinges and sweet aches of only a few minutes earlier weighted her like the infirmities of old age. She went to the closet and pulled out a long white velour robe and shrugged it on.

Catching sight of herself in the mirror, she paused. A faint blue bruise marred the pale column of her neck and one breast bore the pink chafe of Grey's beard. She ran her fingers over the evidence of their passion, wondering at the fact of their existence. They ought to have disappeared, along with Prince Charming. The spell was obviously broken. She wrapped the robe around herself and jerked the belt tight.

She started from the room, but stopped as she passed the chair. Grey had forgotten his tie draped over the back. She picked it up, held it in her hand, and felt the tears she didn't think she had threaten. She squeezed her eyes shut against them and dropped the tie. She wouldn't cry. It wasn't her style.

When she was sure she had her emotions under control, she slid her feet into marabou-trimmed slippers and dragged her way downstairs to the kitchen. Once there, she stared helplessly at the coffee maker, wondering at the power of old habits to drive actions even as the world came to an end. Anything she attempted to put in her stomach would come right back up.

She turned and left the kitchen, wandering aimlessly into the living room. She stared at the chair where Grey had sat and hoped she wouldn't have to sell it before she stopped seeing him there. She turned in a slow circle and saw him everywhere — smelling flowers on the mantel, studying the books on her shelves, standing at the bottom of the stairs smiling up at her.

The sound of the lock on the front door scraping exploded into the melancholy silence. Her hand leaped to her throat and she spun toward the door. She watched the knob turn in paralyzed horror. The door began to open, and her heart beat so loudly in her ears she could hear nothing else.

Chapter Seven

Grey stepped in muttering and kicked the door shut behind him. Balancing a cardboard drink container in one hand and a grease-spotted paper sack in the other, he dropped the ring of keys on the foyer table. Jo stared at him wide-eyed, her capacity for speech momentarily absent.

In his tuxedo, shirt collar open and no longer crisp, and wearing a morning stubble of beard, he should have looked disreputable. Instead, he radiated a rakish bad-boy attractiveness. He glanced up, caught sight of her, and smiled.

"You're up. You were sleeping so soundly when I left, I checked to be sure you were still breathing." His smile took on a teasing glint. "Must have been all the exercise." He nodded toward the key ring. "I dug your keys out of your bag so I wouldn't have to wake you."

Jo made a nondescript noise, hand still at her throat.

"I consider it nothing less than a public service that Cafe du Monde stays open on

New Year's Day. I wasn't the only one there picking up an eye opener. Where's a good place to put this down?"

She waved a hand weakly toward the table in front of the French doors. Grey strode to the table and deposited the bag and carrier, before stepping into the kitchen.

Jo stared at the doorway through which he had disappeared and heard him opening cupboard doors. She followed warily, still unable to believe he was there.

A stack of three plates sat on the counter, while Grey continued to open doors.

"What," Jo began, but her voice cracked. "What," she tried again, "are you looking for?"

Grey peered into the cupboard he had just opened. "Paper napkins. Where do you keep them?"

"I don't use them. I don't have any."

He glanced at her impatiently. "Everyone has paper napkins."

"I don't."

"We can use paper towels instead then." He tore two off the roll mounted above the sink, grabbed the plates and carried them back to the table. He set two of the plates on opposite sides of the table and upended the bag over the third. Sugar-dusted beignets mounded temptingly on it. When he pulled the lids off the two drinks, the aroma of coffee tickled her nose.

Grey looked over his shoulder at her. "Breakfast is served."

Jo's gaze traveled from Grey to the table and back again.

A crease appeared between his brows. "Jo? You okay? It didn't seem to me that you had that much to drink at the party, but maybe I missed something."

He mustn't know. He mustn't ever know what she had been thinking, how devastated she had felt. She shook her head. "I'm just not awake yet." She started for a chair at the table, but Grey stopped her with a hand on her arm.

He took her chin in his hand and tipped her face first one way, then the other. "You do look a little pale. Sure you're okay?"

She tried a smile, found she could manage one. "I'm fine. I just need some of that delicious coffee you brought."

"Good. I'd hate to think all that wild behavior of last night was the result of nothing more than an overindulgence in champagne."

She felt a flush creep up her neck as she moved to sit down. "I wasn't all that wild."

Grey gave a bark of laughter. "Honey, I have the scars to prove otherwise."

Her gaze lifted briefly, then skidded away. "Sorry"

"I'm not." The smile that played around his lips was wicked. "I can't wait for you to hurt me again."

The sip of coffee she had just taken went down the wrong way and she choked.

Grey slapped her back helpfully. "Was it something I said?"

Jo shot him a look. "Cute."

Grey's grin as he dropped into the chair across from her was unrepentant. "Yeah, you are. All the way down to those silly slippers you're wearing."

Jo stuck her foot out to study the white slip-on with the French heel. "What's wrong with my slippers?"

"Nothing. I just said they were cute."

"It was the way you said it."

Grey rolled his eyes. "I bet those are the same slippers you wear when you're here alone, aren't they?"

She nodded, bewildered as to his point.

"See, that's what I mean. For anybody else those would be company slippers. Hidden in the closet would be a pair of fuzzy mules for when they really wanted to be comfortable."

"I'm comfortable now."

"I know that. I've never seen you looking less than perfectly groomed. Your clothes are always in perfect taste, your hair is always perfectly arranged, even your home is perfect. No newspaper clutter, no dirty glasses in the sink, no damp towels in the bathroom. No paper napkins."

Jo set down her coffee and carefully replaced the beignet she had been preparing to bite into on her plate. "Why do I feel like you disapprove?"

"Not disapprove. I'm just wondering about your somewhat obsessive behavior."

There it was. The perfect opening to tell him about her background. Was she courageous enough to take it? She sipped her coffee, stalling as she considered how to begin.

"I told you I moved around a lot?"

"I remember."

"The reason is that I grew up in foster homes. The longest I ever stayed in one place was three years. There was never a lot of extra to go around. Sometimes not even enough. Not enough new clothes, or shoes, or school supplies, or money." Or love.

She looked away from his too perceptive eyes, lost in the memories of her earlier

135

years. "When I got old enough to work, every penny went for necessities. After living with hand-me-downs and leftovers all my life I promised myself that I would have the best I could afford. That if I couldn't be part of a real family, at least when I was in control my surroundings would be as beautiful as I could make them." Her gaze came back to his and her chin lifted challengingly. "And I have."

Grey studied her silently. He had known about the foster homes. Now he knew about Jo. He noted the pride in her voice, understood it. She had done remarkably well for herself. But there was something more she hadn't told him.

"Why were you in foster homes?"

He thought at first she wasn't going to answer him. "I was born in prison. My mother was serving a term for armed robbery. She died there." Her chin went higher, as though daring him to comment.

He wished he could tell her he had known. He ached for her, for the times people had hurt her with their reactions. He didn't intend to be one of them.

"Relax, Jo, and drink your coffee. If you're looking for outraged propriety, I'm the last person who's going to give you that." He lifted his own cup. "But I'm not going to bleed sympathy all over you, either." Sipping, he watched surprise cross her face.

"Why not? It's been my usual experience that people give me one or the other."

That's what he figured. "I don't want to be part of the 'usual' experience. Not in any way. You don't need my sympathy. Your experiences made you the strong person you are today. Without your early challenges, you wouldn't have accomplished half what you have."

"That's a rather callous attitude."

"If you want someone to help you sing a chorus of 'poor me' you've got the wrong man. We all have things to whine about. Sympathy is about the past. Get over it."

Her eyes sparked with temper and he wondered if he had gone too far. "Easy for you to say," she snapped. "The privileged child of privileged parents, growing up with all the advantages money and family could provide. Why shouldn't I have it now?" Her hand made a sweeping motion encompassing the room and its contents.

"You should have whatever you want and can provide for yourself, but don't confuse family with things. Because family is about more than linen napkins and old silver."

"Well, I wouldn't know about that, would I?" she said, her face stiff with hurt. "This is the closest I can come."

Grey was instantly regretful. "Jo, I'm sorry. I didn't mean to attack the way you've chosen to live. It just doesn't seem quite natural to me. Such order, tidiness, perfection. What are you going to do when you have a husband and children?"

"Are you offering?"

His expression must have betrayed his immediate reaction to the idea of marriage.

She laughed dryly. "I thought not."

Grey reflected grimly that he had certainly managed to botch the morning. "Jo, I haven't done this well at all. I'm not usually so clumsy. Forgive me if I hurt you. Actually, I think you're wonderful. I didn't mean to browbeat you."

She shrugged. "I guess you'll just have to take me the way I am. Perfect." Her teasing smile told him she had forgiven him.

"I can handle it." Her golden eyes glowed as warmly as the morning sunlight that shone through the doors beside her and caught in her hair. "And speaking of taking you . . . I'd like to. Again."

He stood, walked around the table to her, and kissed her thoroughly. Her response came with satisfying speed. He drew her out of her chair and pulled her close against him.

"I've been thinking about the problem of the stairs," he said, "and I have the solution."

He bent quickly and wrapped an arm around her thighs, then stood and heaved her body over his shoulder. She gave a startled yelp and he reached up and patted her bottom reassuringly. "Don't worry. I won't drop you." At the round, firm shape of her, his hand lingered to stroke appreciatively.

Her laugh gurgled from behind his back. "I don't remember this from the fairy tales."

"Honey, I'm going to show you things Prince Charming never thought of," he said, starting up the stairs.

By the time the cab driver carried in Jo's suitcase darkness had already fallen. She paid him and added a tip, then locked the gate tiredly behind him. Inside, she kicked off her shoes, then walked around the living room turning on lights.

Her buying trip had been successful, but exhausting. Replacing her entire inventory at once had required all of her stamina and then some. The trip had been worth the effort, though. She had acquired some wonderful pieces for the new store. The brass bed would get center stage while she owned it, but she already had a customer in mind she was sure would love it.

She padded into the kitchen and poured herself a glass of wine. In the living room she sipped the cool Chablis while she flipped through the mail her neighbor had collected and left on the dining table for her. Nothing demanded her immediate attention, so she left the pile to deal with in the morning.

Her answering machine indicated she had several messages. She dropped into the chair beside the telephone and pushed the playback button. There were two calls from friends who were unaware she had been out of town, one from Vivian asking when they could get together for lunch, one from her insurance agent, one from a fellow dealer about a piece she had been searching for.

She sipped her wine and closed her eyes, waiting for the next message. Grcy's voice came, warm and intimate, banishing her tiredness.

"Hi. You're due back today. I've missed you. It's late and I know you're tired, but I'd love to hear from you. You've been on my mind. A lot. I've got a lecture class on Saturday mornings this semester and appointments all afternoon. That doesn't give us much time, but I can manage lunch if you'll meet me on campus. Let me know."

Jo smiled and picked up the telephone, then punched in Grey's number. She hadn't spoken with him in the two weeks she had been gone, needing a break from the intensity of her love for him, needing to know if distance would blunt the edge. If anything it had only honed a sharper blade. As she listened to his phone ring and waited for him to answer, her heartbeat quickened in anticipation.

"Hello."

"Grey, it's Jo. I just got in and got your message. I'd love to meet you for lunch."

"Great. How was the trip? Besides too long?"

Warmed by his words, she described the items she had found for the store, the unpleasant weather in the north, and her happiness at being back home, not the least part of which was knowing she was once again in the same city with Grey. The hectic schedule she had maintained began to catch up with her and she fought to suppress a yawn.

"You should be in bed, honey. I won't keep you any longer. Get lots of rest. You'll need it," he promised, sending pleasant shivers over her skin. He gave her quick directions on where to meet him the following day and said goodbye.

Jo arrived at the Tulane campus early, having left herself plenty of time to find a parking space. A car was just pulling away from the curb as she drove up, so she slid into the vacant spot. Glancing at her watch as she stepped from her car, she found she had time to spare before Grey's class adjourned.

She strolled past the massive stone Romanesque-style buildings of the original campus, remembering her own days of classes there. Although the administrations were separate, Sophie Newcomb College shared part of the campus with Tulane. Jo had always loved the older section. It had such a look of permanence about it, as though it had always stood amidst the ancient trees that surrounded it.

She continued on to the more modern section of the campus and the lecture hall where Grey's class was being held. She paused outside in the hallway and checked her watch again. Fifteen minutes to go.

After a moment's consideration she looked for a rear door to the room.

Opening it quietly, she discovered a large amphitheater seating at least one hundred fifty students. She slipped quickly into one of the empty seats toward the rear, her gaze seeking Grey.

He stood at the front of the large space in dark slacks and gray corduroy blazer. The tie that he wore around the collar of his blue denim shirt had been loosened comfortably. One hand shoved his blazer aside to prop on his hip, while the other emphasized his words.

He hadn't seen her enter. His attention was centered on a student sitting in the front row on the far side of the room.

"Because," Grey was saying, "people are still hungry. If you're a farmer whose crop has failed because there wasn't enough rain that year, your wife and children won't have enough to eat. You take a job helping to excavate nearby ruins working for a pittance. Then someone comes along and offers you more than your farm has ever made in a year if you'll just misappropriate a few of the many grubby objects you dig up."

Grey shrugged. "It's only a few cracked pots, broken tiles. It's illegal, sure. But who's going to know? And your family's well-being is at stake. What would *you* do, Mr. Ingalls?"

Having made his point, Grey turned and paced in the opposite direction, obviously gathering his thoughts. He stopped and looked back toward the students. "Therein lies the problem with trying to suppress the looting of valuable archaeological sites. Who do you go after — the poor peasant who's just trying to feed his family or the indiscriminate European and American collectors who encourage the practice of looting with their support of it?"

Warming to his subject, Grey raised his finger for emphasis. "The African nation of Mali, though one of the poorest on earth, is a rich source of artifacts in the form of masks, fetishes, bronze sculptures, and terra-cotta figures. Despite strict laws imposed by the Mali government, looting goes on unabated."

Grey stopped and directed his attention to a young woman seated four rows from the front who was yawning. "Either I'm boring you, Miss Richmond, or you had a late night last night. I prefer to think it's the latter. Please try to stay awake," he glanced at his watch, "for the next ten minutes if you can."

The girl blushed a deep pink and sank deeper into her seat. "Sorry, Professor Cantrell. Where was that again?"

"Get it from one of your classmates. As I was saying, the trouble with looting is that it breaks up the remains of ancient cultures to the extent that any knowledge and discoveries they may have made, any addition to the universal store of human knowledge they may have contributed is lost forever."

His gaze scanned the room of students, faltering when it encountered Jo. He threw her a quick surprised smile, causing several of the students to turn in an attempt to discover what had caught his attention. Jo smiled back self-consciously and Grey returned to his lecture.

"I would like all of you," he told his students, "to turn in a thousand word essay by a week from today outlining your solution to the problem of looting."

A general groan went up, which Grey grinned at good-naturedly. "If people don't think about problems, they don't come up with answers. Dismissed."

Jo remained seated while the students gathered papers and notebooks and shuffled noisily from the room. At last only she and Grey remained. He walked to the door and closed it, then returned to his former place.

He put both hands on his hips and regarded her coolly. "Miss Flaherty, could I see you down here, please."

She slid from her seat and walked down the aisle toward him, hiding a smile. "I hope my work is satisfactory, Professor Cantrell."

"That remains to be seen."

When she reached him, he drew her into his arms and pulled her close. She turned her face up and he lowered his mouth to hers in the kind of kiss she had been missing for two long weeks. Her mouth opened hungrily and he plunged inside, his tongue stroking sensitive tissue. She moaned weakly and he broke the kiss off and pressed her head into his shoulder. She noticed she wasn't the only one having trouble drawing a steady breath.

"That's definitely A-level work, Miss Flaherty, but maybe you'd better come to my place and work on extra credit to-night."

She leaned back and looked through her lashes at him. "If you think I need it, Professor."

"Not half as much as I do. God, I've missed you, Jo." He hugged her once and set her away from him. "I promised you lunch. If we don't get out of here, I'm going to come up with a new use for this auditorium."

He ushered her out of the building and along the short walk to the faculty parking area where he had left his car. "Lunch is going to be nothing fancy. It's a fifties-style diner close to the campus that makes great burgers and shakes."

"Sounds okay with me. I just wanted to be with you."

He leaned over and planted another kiss on her mouth. "I don't know how I'm going to wait until tonight," he told her, before backing the car out.

At the diner, noise echoed cheerfully around the black and white space punctuated by chrome and red vinyl. Frankie Avalon crooned in the background, and the waitress, clad in a short full skirt and saddle shoes, popped her gum loudly as she took their orders for hamburgers. She left and Jo smiled in amusement. "It's certainly a popular place," she commented, referring to the crowd that consisted of all ages.

"It may be gimmicky, but they do make the best burgers in town."

The waitress returned with two large chocolate shakes and produced straws with a flourish. Jo inserted hers through the thick, rich ice cream and took a sip. "Mmm, I can't remember when I last had

147

one of these." She stirred with the straw and put her lips to it again. "Definitely worth the calories."

A surge of activity a few tables away caught their attention. The waiters and waitresses assembled around a table of boisterous young girls who looked about ten years old. One of the waitresses carried a small cake bearing one candle behind her back.

"Look, Grey. A birthday party."

Jo smiled as the chorus of help sang a rousing version of "Happy Birthday," before the waitress produced the cake and placed it before a beaming little girl. She struck a match, lit the candle, and waited for the girl to blow it out. Watching her, Jo grew wistful.

"I never had one of those," she said.

"One of those what?"

"A birthday party."

"You're kidding."

"No. Parties are expensive. I had a cake once, though. One of the foster mothers I stayed with baked it for me. It had plain white frosting and those colored sprinkles, and I thought it was the most beautiful thing I'd ever seen."

"I'm sorry life wasn't better for you, Jo."

She shrugged and smiled. "Don't be.

There were good times, too."

"Tell me about one."

Jo chuckled, remembering. "It wasn't humorous at the time, but it seems so now. I was invited to a birthday party for a girl in my class. Her mother made her invite everyone. We were probably about the age of those girls over there. Anyway, after the cake and ice cream and present opening, the mother snatched her daughter up and said it was time for the birthday spanking. She asked all of us to help her count the spanks. That little girl laughed louder than anybody. I probably looked like my eyes were about to fall out of my head. I'd never heard of a birthday spanking, and the idea of getting hit and thinking it was funny was as shocking as anything I'd ever seen. For the rest of the party I made sure to stay as far away from that little girl's mother as possible." Her smile invited him to share the joke.

He grinned and shook his head sadly. "No birthday spankings, either? You really were a deprived child."

"I may not have gotten birthday spankings, but there were plenty of the other kind."

Grey grasped her hand. "I apologize, Jo."

She met his gaze, surprised. "What for?

It wasn't your fault."

"No. I apologize for my previous remarks about your childhood, for not being more understanding. You must have thought I was a pompous ass."

"You made me mad, but inside I knew you were right. Sometimes I do have a tendency to feel sorry for myself. Not often, but it's there. You said the best thing you could have."

"Thank you for being such a special person. You're more gracious than I deserve." He carried her hand to his lips and pressed a kiss to her knuckles.

Her mouth went suddenly dry. The arrival of the waitress with their hamburgers saved her from having to speak. She took back her hand and swallowed.

Grey nonchalantly picked up his burger and took a bite. Jo followed suit, wondering if he knew the effect he had on her. Didn't he know that in the twenty-first century men didn't go around kissing ladies' hands?

They finished eating, and Grey signaled for their check. "I'm sorry to rush you, Jo, but I need to get back."

"That's all right. After being away two weeks I've got lots to catch up on, too."

"Do you mind if we run by my apartment on the way back? There are some papers there I need."

"Of course not. Besides, I haven't seen your home yet. I'm curious."

Grey's apartment turned out to be located in a modern high-rise condominium. Jo registered surprise as he led her into his minimally furnished contemporary apartment. Gray carpeting in a darker shade than the walls covered the floor and built in seating units. The few paintings were starkly abstract.

"It's not quite what I expected," she said.

"I think I bought it in a fit of rebellion against the atmosphere I grew up with. It's beginning to pall on me, but not enough to go to the trouble of looking for something else. It's close to my work, so at least it's convenient. Make yourself at home while I find those papers."

He had invited, so after he left the room she did just that. Glass shelves inset in one wall held a fascinating array of objects and she walked over for a closer look. Her gaze fell first on a bronze horse sculpture that looked to be very old Chinese. It shared space with a red-painted ceramic bowl of clearly early vintage, but she couldn't pinpoint the origin.

A wide red and blue beaded collar similar to those found in Egyptian tombs made her fingers itch to pick it up and hold it to her own neck. Intimidated by its obvious age, she settled for stroking the beads delicately with a fingertip. Close by stood a small clay statue so obviously female as to be obscene. Its huge, pendulous breasts and swollen belly faintly repelled Jo and she moved on quickly.

Pride of place was occupied by a small, obviously old, pottery vessel that sat in a glass case atop a carpeted pedestal. She peered at it closely, curious as to why it had been accorded such treatment. A crack ran down the length of one side and there were several large chips out of it.

"Admiring my treasure? I knew you had great taste." Grey had returned, a file folder grasped in his hand.

"What is it?"

"A frankincense container. Closest estimates place it between two and four thousand years old."

Jo's eyes widened and she turned back to study it again. The thought occurred that the object must have been very expensive. In fact, all the items she had been looking at must have been very expensive. Did a college professor's salary allow for collecting such treasures? Remembering Grey's earlier lecture to his students, she wondered disturbingly if it was even legal to own some of the artifacts that graced Grey's living room.

"Where did you get it?" she asked, striving to keep suspicion from her mind and voice.

"I led a dig in Oman about five years ago that discovered two previously unknown ancient trading sites for frankincense. The container was a gift from the Omani government."

His explanation sounded plausible enough. "It must be valuable. Shouldn't it be in a vault somewhere?"

"But then I couldn't enjoy it. I get a kick out of looking at it and wondering about the frankincense it held — what its ultimate destiny was."

"Its destiny?"

"The Egyptians used the stuff for embalming. The Pharaohs believed that burning it allowed them to commune with the gods. It was also used at most religious ceremonies and cremations. That little jar could have contributed to King Tut's embalming or Nero's funeral. It's like looking at history."

Jo looked at the container with new respect. "And to think, I used to believe that Louis XIV made something old."

Grey smiled. "It all depends on your perspective. You ready to go?"

He drove Jo to her car. Before she could step from the Mustang, he stopped her with a hand on her knee. "Can I pick you up for dinner tonight?"

She smiled provocatively. "You'd better."

His eyes returned the smile. "Wear something casual. Dinner's just an excuse."

"I know."

Chapter Eight

That evening Grey slid into the driver's seat beside her, inserted the key into the ignition, then leaned over Jo and pressed his mouth to hers, the kiss long, deep, and hungry. By the time he raised his head he could hear his own heartbeat thudding in his ears.

"How do you feel about Chinese?" he asked thickly.

Jo opened her eyes slowly, looking bemused. "Communist or Taiwanese?"

"Food."

"Oh. Love it."

Grey turned the key and started the engine. "Good. There's an entire take-out meal sitting on my kitchen counter right now. We can be there in twenty minutes."

"That long?"

Grey nosed his car into traffic and slanted a quick look at her. "Lady, I like the way your mind works."

Twenty-five minutes later Grey unlocked the door of his apartment. He had left the lights on and jazz playing on the stereo, since he hoped to be coming right back.

They walked in, his hand at her waist, and he closed the door behind them. "Come here," he growled and gathered Jo in his arms before she had taken two steps.

His mouth came down hard and Jo returned the kiss with gratifying urgency, her lips parting eagerly to accept his tongue. He plunged inside and she moaned, holding tight to him. His hands pressed her high against his pelvis. At the needy sounds she made, he grew even harder.

He wrenched his mouth from hers with an effort. "How hungry are you?" he asked hoarsely, giving her a last chance to slow things down.

"Starving." She pulled his mouth back to hers and arched her breasts against his chest.

What control he had snapped. He shoved her against the wall and pinned her there, grinding his hips into her yielding softness. His hands skimmed up and down her sides, molding her curves, while her seeking mouth tipped first one way, then the other, deepening the kiss. She lifted her legs clad in clinging ivory knit and wrapped their length around his waist.

He pushed off from the wall and lurched down the hall, Jo clinging as though she had been grafted to him. In the bedroom, he set her down and quickly stripped her out of her leggings and long matching sweater. The sight of her in a white lace bra and tiny scrap of panties gave him pause. Her pale skin glowed through the lace, her hard, puckered nipples deep pink against the white. Looking at her, he felt his erection strain at the fly of his jeans.

She lifted her hands to unfasten her bra, but Grey stopped her. "No. I want to do that."

He yanked his sweater off over his head, jerked down his zipper, and shucked jeans and briefs together. When he was naked, he turned back to Jo. "Now you."

He reached around her and unhooked her bra, before drawing it away. Her breasts, freed from their confinement, thrust forward, begging for attention. Grey grasped either side of her waist and lifted her straight up until her breasts were level with his mouth. He took a nipple into his mouth and she gasped and braced her hands on his shoulders, arching her head back. He suckled first one breast and then the other, pleased at the moans she emitted.

"Please, Grey, put me down," she panted. "I want to touch you too."

He let her slide slowly down the length

of his body, torturing them both with the sensations of flesh against flesh. Her feet had barely touched the floor, when he dropped to the bed, drawing her down with him.

He reached across her, opened a drawer in the nightstand, and extracted a condom. After putting it on, he turned to her, covering her with his body, and sought out her mouth. His tongue went deep and his hand skated over her belly to the mound barely covered by a whisper of lace.

She mewed and tipped her pelvis up. "Please, Grey. You don't have to wait. I'm ready now."

He rose on his knees and drew the panties off down her long legs, before pressing her thighs apart and kneeling between them. His fingers found her already wet and as ready as she had promised. He stroked her once to open her, then scooped his hands under her and started to lift her hips to meet his mouth.

Jo's eyes went wide and she grasped his arms, fingernails digging in. "Grey, no, wait," she breathed. "I don't — I've never —"

He paused, decided her hesitation was more nerves than fear. "So now you will." His eyes gave her a moment's warning, before he lifted her and lowered his head.

His tongue touched her lightly and she cried out. He let it circle her tender flesh, flick teasingly, then dip deep to savor the feminine taste of her. Her fingers tightened on his arms, nails digging even deeper, but he knew she had no thoughts of stopping him. Her head tossed on the pillow and her soft whimpers were almost continuous.

He wasn't sure how much longer he could wait. His tongue thrust deeply into her, pushing her over the edge, and her body went taut as a bow. Her voice sobbed out in a high keening cry as she arched against his mouth.

When her spasms slowed, he moved over her and entered her in one swift stroke, driving her back up. She answered his thrusts with her own, bucking wildly, her nails raking frantically across his back. When the second climax hit her she screamed, taking him with her.

Afterward, she lay on her stomach, sprawled limply, one leg between his own, her belly against his hip. Her head rested on his shoulder and her contented sighs feathered over his chest. He combed gentle fingers absentmindedly through her damp hair, still stunned himself. He couldn't remember sharing lovemaking as intense as what he had just experienced with any other woman. Jo's trust, after her early sexual encounter, humbled him.

He wondered what she was thinking, was afraid to ask. If she gave voice to her feelings, then he would be forced to deal with them. He didn't want to have to consider the future. The present was challenge enough.

Over the music playing quietly in the living room, he heard her stomach growl and laughed. "Romantic," he teased dryly.

She propped herself up on an elbow and smiled sheepishly. "You did mention dinner."

"I did. Let's get some food into you. Can't have you getting weak from hunger. The evening's young yet."

A few minutes later they were seated at Grey's glass and marble dining table eating out of an assortment of cartons. He wore a dark blue dressing gown, while his wine-red velour robe several sizes too big for Jo wrapped her adorably. She looked like a little girl, until he remembered the very womanly body underneath.

Jo poked in the carton of cashew chicken searching for the last morsel of meat. She popped it into her mouth and washed it down with a sip of the wine Grey had poured, before shoving the carton away from her. "That's it. I'm done."

"You haven't had your fortune cookie yet. Tradition demands that you finish a Chinese meal with a fortune cookie." He pushed one across the table to her.

"I certainly wouldn't want to break with tradition," she said, picking up the cookie and snapping it open. She extracted the slip of paper and straightened it to read, "You will have strong sons and beautiful daughters." She had always hoped, planned for sons and daughters — well, maybe just one of each — and since meeting Grey those hazy, half-formed images of children that lived in her dreams had acquired sable-brown hair and eyes the color of the sky.

She had tried determinedly to forget Grey's attitude toward marriage. If a reminder intruded, she told herself firmly there was a chance he would change. Otherwise being with him hurt too much. And there would be no children by Grey outside of marriage. She wouldn't bring a child into the world under those conditions, and Grey was religiously careful about using protection.

Under the circumstances, the words typed on the small piece of paper struck her as especially poignant. She was appalled to find tears stinging her eyes and looked down quickly, praying Grey hadn't seen.

No such luck.

"Jo? Honey, what's wrong?"

She could just imagine Grey's reaction if she told him she was crying because she wanted to marry him and have his children. What man wouldn't blanch and run?

His hand reached across the table and tipped her chin up. "You can tell me."

Right, of course she could. Grey was too perceptive to put off with a blatant lie. She searched her mind frantically for a reason that would sound convincing. A modified version of the truth would carry a ring of believability.

She blinked the tears away and forced a smile. "I'm twenty-nine. I always thought by this time I would have a family. The business used up so much of my life I never got around to it."

"Honey, you make twenty-nine sound like one step away from Medicare. You've still got plenty of time."

"I know." She lifted a shoulder. "The fortune just caught me by surprise. I'm okay, honest."

"Sure?"

"Yes. You didn't read your fortune. Let's

see what the future holds in store for you."

He opened his own cookie and quickly scanned the words on the paper ribbon, before giving a laugh and tossing the paper to Jo. She picked it up curiously and saw with surprise the fortunes were identical.

"Whoever is in charge of writing these things must lack for imagination," Grey commented. He focused on something behind her for a moment and a smile creased his cheek. "But just to be on the safe side, maybe you'd better sit in a different chair."

Jo glanced around to see what he had been looking at. The nasty little clay statue of a woman squatted on the shelf behind her, its eyes seeming to bore into Jo's skull. She grimaced and turned back. "Why do you say that?"

Grey tipped his head toward the statue. "That's a fertility goddess from early Nigeria."

Jo twisted back to look at the statue again. "It's creepy. Why would you want something that ugly around?"

Grey studied the figure, a fond expression in his eyes. "I've never considered her ugly. Maybe because I'm concentrating on the culture that created her, and what she represented to them."

"Is she valuable?"

"She certainly was to the Nigerians."

"No. I mean the statue. Should you have her here? What if she were stolen?"

Grey's mouth slanted sardonically. "Then the thief would have a very good copy. She's a reproduction. The original is in the Smithsonian. Most of these," he indicated the other items that Jo had noted earlier, "are museum reproductions. I couldn't afford the originals, even if they were available. And in museums they're there for everyone. How incredibly selfish it would be to keep them just for myself."

"What about the frankincense container?"

He appeared chagrined. "Practice what you preach? Actually there are several examples in much better condition than mine already in museums. I thought it would be forgivable to keep this one." He grinned. "And I wanted it."

Jo laughed. "At least you're honest."

The smile left his face and his expression became unreadable. He reached for the wine bottle and refilled their glasses, then stood and picked up his. "Let's go sit in front of the fire."

Jo was left to stare at his back as he crouched in front of the fireplace, igniting the modern gas logs. She picked up her glass and followed him. After adjusting the flame, he straightened and moved to the couch, sat and patted the spot next to him. She dropped beside him and curled her feet under her. Grey stretched his legs out and propped them, ankles crossed, on the coffee table.

Jo sipped her wine, content to sit quietly with Grey, feeling his nearness and listening to the music. After a few minutes, she dropped her head tiredly onto his shoulder. His hand came up to cup her cheek briefly and she closed her eyes.

She hadn't realized she had begun to doze until she felt her glass being removed from her fingers. She came awake with a start.

"It's all right. Go ahead and sleep for a while," Grey told her gently. He leaned across her and turned out the lamp on the end table. Humor laced his voice as he added, "I promise not to start anything without you."

She smiled faintly and closed her eyes again. She hadn't realized how tired she was. Grey's shoulder felt so warm and solid, and she snuggled into it gratefully.

The noise was tremendous and she stared in horror as Riverwalk collapsed with her children — hers and Grey's — trapped inside. She screamed and began digging frantically through the wreckage to reach them. No matter how hard or fast she dug, she couldn't seem to get any closer to them. She cried in anguish and batted impatiently at the hands that tried to prevent her from digging any further.

"Jo! Jo, wake up."

She realized the hands were Grey's. "Oh, Grey, thank God you're here! The children —"

"Jo, you're dreaming. Wake up, honey."

She became aware of being gently shaken and opened her eyes to find Grey frowning at her. She sat up straight and pushed her hair off her face with a hand that trembled.

"You were having a nightmare," Grey said, a line still between his brows.

Jo drew a shuddering breath and pressed her hand to her chest. Her heart still pounded hard enough to gallop away. "You've got *that* right. Thank God."

Grey's brows arched in disbelief. "That you had a nightmare?"

"No, that that's all it was." She reached for her wineglass and took a quick gulp. "It was so awful."

"Want to tell me about it?"

She opened her mouth to do just that, then closed it again. "No."

166

Grey appeared nonplused. "Why not?"

In spite of the effects she still felt from the emotional fire drill, she almost smiled. People probably didn't tell him "no" very often. "Because."

"Because? What kind of reason is that?"

"A woman's."

He turned his eyes heavenward. "And they accuse men of being sexist."

"I don't."

"Good thing. You wouldn't have a leg to stand on." He noted her glass was empty. "You want some more of that?"

She needed distance. The dream had left her too vulnerable. If she didn't get away from Grey for a while, she feared giving away more of herself than he was ready for or wanted. "No, I'd better not. I really do need to get home. I have to get up early tomorrow."

"Jo, tomorrow is Sunday."

"I know, but I have so much to do, after being gone, getting the new location ready. I have several pieces that will be arriving soon and I want to be able to put them in place right away."

His gaze skimmed over her, heating those places where it lingered. It lighted on her mouth, and her lips tingled as surely as though he had kissed her. "I can't persuade you to stay a little longer?" he asked warmly.

"You could, so don't try. Please."

He gave a rueful smile. "That's some trick, pumping my ego and making me feel guilty all at the same time. Okay. I'll restrain myself, but you'd better get dressed pronto. I've been imagining unwrapping that robe for the past hour. I don't handle disappointment very well."

She didn't either. At Grey's words she almost changed her mind. Thinking about him peeling the robe from her body and making love to her by the firelight provided a strong inducement to stay. Her gaze sought his and her lips parted, unconsciously inviting him to cover them with his own.

His hand grasped her upper arm and pushed her up from the couch. "Go. I'll wait out here while you dress. If I don't, you'll never have the chance to put on a stitch."

Jo dressed quickly in the leggings and sweater she had worn earlier and dug in her purse for a hairbrush. As she stroked it through her hair in front of the mirror, she noticed, dismayed, that one of her earrings was missing. She searched the dresser top, but didn't find it.

The diamond studs were the first quality jewelry she had bought herself when she could afford extras. They represented much more than just their replacement value. The possibility she had lost one upset her more than the loss of a recent purchase costing twice as much would.

She shook out the bedding, looked under the pillows, and knelt to search under the bed, all without success. She told herself to stay calm, the earring had to be in the room somewhere. Thinking back, she decided it probably came off when Grey pulled her sweater over her head. It could have snagged in the knit.

She walked back to where she had been standing at the time and knelt, then examined the carpet with her fingers. They brushed over something hard and she stopped to find what it was they touched. The back of the earring. That meant the rest of it had to be nearby.

She continued searching, but turned up nothing. The dresser was close. Maybe the earring had bounced or rolled that far. She lay on her stomach and tried to see in the dark space underneath, but it was too dim. She stretched her arm gingerly under the dresser, glad Grey seemed to be a reasonably fastidious housekeeper. She wasn't likely to encounter any creatures more threatening than dust bunnies.

She rubbed her hand carefully along the floor and suddenly felt the stud. Her fingers closed triumphantly around it and she quickly withdrew her hand from beneath the dresser, but in her haste snagged her sleeve. The object she had snagged it on, a manila envelope taped along its outer edges, came out along with her arm, the tape on one edge stuck to her sweater.

She pulled the tape from the wool knit and dropped the envelope on the floor in order to replace the earring in her earlobe. After securing the stud, she picked up the envelope and studied it, a puzzled frown drawing her brows together.

It appeared to have been taped to the underside of the dresser until she had dislodged it in her search. No address had been written on it. She turned it over and noted the flap was unsealed. Shushing the little voice that told her she was being nosy, she lifted the flap and looked inside.

Money. A lot of it.

She stared at it incredulously, waiting for her brain to register what her eyes saw. Her thumb shuffled the bills, not a one under a hundred dollars and most over. She tried to compute the amount, but gave up. She only knew that she held in her hand well over ten thousand dollars.

Why would Grey have had that kind of cash hidden in his apartment? Why not have the money in a bank? She didn't like any of the answers that came immediately to mind.

She wasn't aware of making the decision to keep from Grey her discovery of the money, but she found herself back on the floor restoring the envelope to what she hoped was its original location. If she had shown the money to Grey, he would have had a perfectly reasonable explanation for its presence. Of course he would.

The thoughts and possibilities chasing each other around in her head were making her sick. Grey was a good man. She'd never known one better. But good people didn't stash huge amounts of cash in hidey-holes in their homes. Or did they? How much did she know really about what anybody else did? She should just ask him right out about the envelope, he would give her the perfectly reasonable explanation, and the whole matter would be cleared up easily. But what if it wasn't?

Her faith in Grey's innate integrity had taken a punch, but it was still standing. She wouldn't test it further. Whatever

Grey was involved in was his business. She had no right to meddle. He was a competent individual and could work things out.

Grey rapped loudly on the door. "If you don't hurry," he called, "I'm going to come in and persuade you to stay after all."

Jo ran to the door and pulled it open, greeting him with a smile that she was sure betrayed the guilt she couldn't help feeling. "I'm ready."

His gaze traveled down her length and back up. "Too bad. Give me five minutes to throw some clothes on and I'll run you home." A smile lit his eyes. "Unless you'd like to stay and help."

Jo tried to respond naturally to his teasing, forcing awareness of the money deep into the back of her mind. "I think I'll wait in the living room."

"Spoil sport."

She patted his cheek on the way out. "Don't pout. It isn't worthy of Prince Charming."

Chapter Nine

Jo surveyed the store with satisfaction. She had liked the previous shop, but the new one exceeded even her optimistic expectations. The walls, rag-rolled in rich ochre paint glowed golden in the late afternoon light, and the polished wood floors set off the gently faded antique rugs to perfection. Not all of the furniture was in place yet, but she could visualize the end result.

She was surprised to see what a good foil the wall color proved to be for paintings and artwork. Sarah had assured her it would be all right, but Jo had retained doubts. As it turned out, Sarah had been completely vindicated.

"It looks good, Jo."

Jo turned to Sarah, who stood beside her checking out their joint effort, and smiled. "Thanks in large part to you. I appreciate what a great job you've done."

"No thanks necessary. You'll be getting my bill in a few days."

"Your services were worth every penny." Faced with a large echoing space whose decor had consisted of fluorescent lights and avocado green carpet, Jo panicked then remembered Grey's sister had offered to help design the new shop. When she called Sarah, the woman had greeted her warmly and agreed with alacrity to assist Jo in getting the store ready.

Their only disagreement had been over payment. Sarah had wanted to do it as a courtesy, but Jo insisted on paying Sarah her regular fee. If Sarah didn't agree to bill her, Jo refused to allow her to set foot in the place.

Sarah had finally given in with a laugh. "You drive a hard bargain, Jo."

Over the course of the month's work the two women had become close friends. Although Jo was excited about finally being able to reopen, she would miss the frequent meetings with Sarah to discuss business. Once the business matter had been taken care of, they had found any number of other things to talk about. They had hashed over everything from work to clothes to men to one man in particular.

Jo hadn't intended to tell Sarah how much she really cared for Grey, but finally admitted to it after persistent, friendly prying on Sarah's part. Sarah made no secret of the fact that she'd love to see Jo and

Grey marry, but even she doubted Grey would ever take that step again. "Although," Sarah had told her, "you're the first woman he's brought to a family dinner. Could be promising."

"Sarah, please don't say anything to Grey. I'd die if he got the idea he was being pressured."

Sarah had simply laughed. "Not to worry. No one pressures Grey to do anything he doesn't want to do. He's been that way since he was a little boy. It used to give the folks fits. Grey only obeyed those rules *he* thought were reasonable. The rest he just ignored. No amount of punishment or restrictions could gain his co-operation. Trust me, he won't propose just because somebody else thinks it's a good idea."

"I'm not afraid he'll propose against his will. I'm afraid if he knew how much I love him it would make him uncomfortable."

"So? Who cares if he's uncomfortable?"

"I do. If he starts to worry that I'll be hurt, he's liable to break things off all together. That's the way his mind works."

"Hmm. You're probably right. You already know him pretty well. He's basically a nice man. Convoluted reasoning though it seems, he *would* think it was for your own good to stop seeing you. Men." Her delicate snort expressed her opinion of the sex clearly.

"So you won't say anything to him?"

The young woman appeared to be thinking over the options.

"Sarah?"

"All right, all right. But it just kills me that he can't see you're the best thing that's ever happened to him. I don't think a nudge in the right direction would come amiss, but I won't be the one to do it. Of course I can't speak for Vivian or Andrea. They happen to share my opinion."

Jo hadn't realized how much Grey's family liked her. The knowledge warmed her immeasurably. "Thank you for the vote of confidence and the moral support. It means a lot."

Sarah had given her a quick hug. "Hey it's the least I can do. You're my new best friend, and I hope one day you'll be my sister-in-law."

Jo smiled, remembering the conversation, and glanced at her new best friend. At the moment Sarah was chewing on her lip while she studied the room. Finally she nodded. "Yup, it's done."

"I thought we had already established that."

"I like to make sure all the finishing

touches are in. After all, it's my work out there. I'm hoping you'll recommend me to customers who comment on the decor."

"That goes without saying."

"I think a little celebration is in order about now. Wait right here." Sarah hurried into the small room they had enclosed in the back of the store and returned minutes later carrying a bottle of chilled champagne, two flutes, and a plate of petit fours. "*Voilà*, a celebration."

"Where did all this come from?" Jo asked in pleased surprise.

"I swung by after lunch and stashed it in the refrigerator. See, I told you that little thing would come in handy."

"But I distinctly remember that you mentioned how convenient it would be for keeping salad and yogurt, not champagne and fat pills."

"See, already we're coming up with new uses for it." Sarah set the articles on the antique desk that already held a state-of-the-art cash register and proceeded to uncork the bottle.

They were settled cozily in two down-cushioned armchairs, the champagne and petit fours on a butler's tray-table between them when there was a knock on the door.

"Just ignore it," Sarah advised. "You've already got a sign in the window announcing you'll be open on Monday."

"I'd better not. It might be someone important." Jo heaved herself up and slipped her feet back into the shoes she had kicked off earlier. Her heels alternately clicked over bare floor and whispered across precious rugs as she walked to the door. By the time she reached it, she saw through the glass that her caller was Grey. He stood on the doorstep dressed in dark slacks, sweater, and bomber jacket, looking casual and appealing.

She pulled the door open and smiled. "Grey, what a nice surprise."

"I finished up early today. Sarah's office said you were both here, so I thought I'd run over. You told me the work was about finished. How'd it turn out?"

Jo stepped back and held the door wider. "Come in and see for yourself."

Grey stepped in and arched his brow at the glass of champagne Jo had forgotten she still held. "Nice work if you can get it," he commented.

Jo laughed. "Sarah brought it to celebrate. Come have some." She led Grey to the furniture grouping that formed the small sitting area she and Sarah had claimed.

Grey's sister looked up from the petit four she was considering. "I thought you said it might be someone important," she told Jo.

"It is, squirt," Grey informed her. "Show the proper respect."

Sarah patted manicured fingers over a yawn.

Jo observed the exchange with amusement, knowing how much love was shared by the siblings. Grey turned his back on Sarah and studied the store, his gaze taking in all the improvements that had been made.

"Nice job, sis."

"Such effusiveness. Please, Greydon, you'll embarrass me."

"Not yet but keep it up and I might."

Sarah held up her hand in surrender. "Uncle. Want some champagne?"

He eyed the plate of delicate cakes. "Not if I'm interrupting a girls-only chatfest."

"Oh, stay," Sarah urged. "We're discussing the perfidy of males. It'll be fun."

Grey directed a warning look at her. "Perhaps I misunderstood your uncle."

"Just ignore her," Jo said. "I'll see if I can find another glass." The only thing she was able to scrounge up in the back room was a leftover Styrofoam coffee cup she rinsed out.

"It's not very elegant," she apologized when she returned. "Here, Grey, you take my glass and I'll use this."

"Don't be ridiculous. The cup is fine. The champagne will taste just as good."

Jo seriously doubted that but the issue wasn't worth arguing about. She poured a generous amount into the cup while Grey pulled up another chair and settled his large frame in it. Taking the cup from her, he nodded his thanks and sipped.

"The place really is a beauty, Jo. You have cause to celebrate."

"Thanks. Although most of it is Sarah's doing. The grand reopening is Monday. You're going to be here, aren't you?" She watched a shadow come and go behind his eyes and wondered at its cause.

"I'll sure try, but I can't make any promises."

Jo tried to mask her disappointment and asked brightly why he was off early.

"An appointment I had canceled out on me."

"A student?"

His gaze lifted from his cup, and there was a beat of silence before he spoke. "Yeah."

"I wish we'd known you were coming," Sarah said. "We sent the help home, then decided we weren't completely happy with the furniture arrangement. We spent two hours muling this stuff into place."

"If you had waited, I'd have been glad to help. Shoving furniture around would have been at least as productive as what I spent the afternoon doing."

"Shoving?" Sarah looked appalled. "On these floors, I think not."

"Of course. What was I thinking?" He glanced around at the larger pieces. "In any case, you two shouldn't be trying to move these things. They're too heavy."

"Now there's a news flash," Sarah said dryly.

"Since you're here now," Jo said, "maybe you can help us with one thing."

"Sure."

"See that brass bed over there."

Grey looked. "You mean the one that looks like a birdcage?"

"Does it?" Jo tipped her head and studied the ornate scrollwork and the posts that curled upward to form a canopy shaped like a crown. "I guess it does at that. Anyway, I'd like it turned to face in a different direction. If you take one end and Sarah and I take the other, we should be able to do it."

"No problem." He put down his cup and approached the bed, Jo and Sarah on his heels.

Grey rested his hands on his hips and looked it over, his gaze traveling up the posts to the canopy and back down. "Pretty sexy. Is it French?"

"Uh huh."

"Figures." His expression turned speculative. "Be a shame to sell it before we give it a trial run."

"Grey!" Jo hissed. She jerked her head toward Sarah.

"Don't mind me. I'll just be a little mouse in the corner," Sarah assured her with a laugh. "But he does have a point. I've been eyeing this thing myself. Maybe you should consider renting it out," she suggested, her expression droll.

"I'd be grateful right now if you'd just help me move it," Jo told her repressively.

"Boy, are you stuffy," Sarah complained as she and Jo grasped the rail at the foot of the bed.

"No." Grey corrected, getting a grip on the headboard. "I can assure you she's not." He smiled suggestively and Jo felt a sweet tug in her belly.

"Do tell?" Sarah smirked, the brows reaching for her hairline promising questions later.

Jo's smile trembled at the corners of her lips. "Just pick up the damn bed, okay?"

Jo totaled the day's receipts at the close of business Wednesday, happy with the beginnings the business was making. She had been worried that the present location wouldn't be as lucrative as the one at Riverwalk had been, but her concerns were proving unfounded. While she had lots of drop-in traffic at Riverwalk, the shoppers on Magazine Street tended to be more serious buyers.

She walked to the doors, intending to lock up for the day, but two men entered before she could do so. They both wore dark conservative suits, although the shorter of the two had broken out with a subtly patterned tie in blues and greens that seemed wildly radical compared to the navy trousers and jacket.

The taller man, whose blond hair was brushed back from an angular face, reached into an inside pocket and extracted a wallet. He opened it and flashed identification for her. "Miss Flaherty?"

At her nod, he continued. "I'm Agent Brannigan with the U.S. Customs Service. This is Agent Kernan. We'd like to speak with you if it's convenient. It shouldn't take long."

She wondered how Agent Brannigan

would react if she told him it really *wasn't* convenient. She understood the courtesy was strictly a formality. He intended to speak with her whether it was convenient or not.

"Now is fine. What did you want to talk to me about?" She tried to remember the last trip she had taken out of the country. England. She was sure she had declared everything required by law. Besides, did Customs hunt you down over a bottle of perfume?

"We are currently investigating the smuggling of illegal antiquities. We know they're coming through the Caribbean and into New Orleans. From here they're being dispersed to various locations. Pieces have been recovered from as far away as New York and Los Angeles."

She wasn't ignorant of the practice, especially after listening to Grey's comments on it. "What kinds of things are you talking about?"

"Most notably items from Africa and the Middle East. In addition to U.S. laws prohibiting the import of antiquities stolen from other countries, there are currently trade bans in effect against certain areas."

"I don't understand what all this has to do with me. As you can see I don't carry anything of that nature."

"We're speaking with all the major antique dealers in the city. There's the chance that collectors of these items may contact one of you in an effort to acquire more. It's also not unlikely that you may come across one of the smuggled items."

He removed a card from his wallet and handed it to her. "If that happens we would appreciate your calling us. I can be reached at this number any time. Don't hesitate to use it if something seems suspicious to you."

She took the card and studied it for a moment before dropping it on her desk. "I'll certainly do that, Agent Brannigan, but I don't really think it will be necessary. I've never come across anything like what you've mentioned in all the years I've been in business."

"You never can tell. Thank you for your time."

Jo followed the men to the door and locked it behind them thoughtfully. It was oddly coincidental she should hear from them, when Grey had so recently spoken about the problem of smuggling. Incidents came to mind that she had all but forgotten. Each one by itself hadn't warranted a second thought, but taken as a whole they began to form an ominous pattern starting as far back as his presence in her store to begin with. Grey didn't even like antiques.

She hated having suspicions about Grey, but once started down the track, the runaway train refused to be halted. If Grey were somehow involved in the smuggling, then a lot of previously mysterious things suddenly made sense. And there were all those artifacts in his apartment. He said they were reproductions, but how would she know? They had looked real enough to her. Had the frankincense container really been a gift of the Omani government?

Her stomach churned at the thought Grey might have lied to her. She had never been as open with a man, as vulnerable to him as with Grey. She never would be again, if her trust had been misplaced.

The money. The final damning piece of evidence. She didn't imagine smugglers took checks or plastic. The cash was used to buy the items. Or perhaps it was money he made dealing in them. The specifics were difficult to nail down, but she knew the truth lay somewhere close.

She walked back to the desk with leaden feet and picked up the card she had dropped. What should she do? Tell Grey what she knew and give him an opportunity to explain? There was always the slim chance she was wrong — that the two of them would laugh about her suspicions later.

Or perhaps he wouldn't laugh. Perhaps he would feel betrayed, even hurt, that she suspected him for even a moment. He spoke so eloquently against the practice of looting other cultures. Could he speak so sincerely about the subject if he were participating in the very activity he condemned? Was his zeal genuine or just part of a cover?

The questions hammered at her relentlessly as she drove home, kept her company through a listless dinner, and followed her into the shower she took in an effort to relax. When she stepped out and grabbed a towel, she was no closer to the answers than she'd been hours earlier. She dried off and wrapped her hair in a second towel, donned her robe, and padded downstairs.

She had just poured herself a glass of wine when the telephone rang. She considered letting the machine handle the call, but she had never been able to ignore the compelling summons of a ringing phone. At the last second she lifted the receiver and answered. "Hello?"

"Hi, honey, it's Grey."

Her mind went blank. How should she respond? All she could think about was the visit from the two agents earlier in the day.

At her silence Grey spoke again. "You're upset with me."

How had he found out already?

"You have a right to be," he continued. "I'm sorry I couldn't make your official opening."

The Customs agents' appearance had driven everything else from her mind. She had forgotten her hurt and disappointment of Monday afternoon, when it become obvious Grey wasn't going to show. She waited for a call that evening explaining why, but none had come. Grey didn't owe her an accounting of his schedule every minute of the day, but she had thought they were close enough he would have realized how important Monday was to her.

"I really wanted to make it, but something came up that I couldn't get out of."

Not even long enough to find a phone? She waited for him to go on, to elaborate, but he added nothing to what he had said. Unwilling to let him know his absence had hurt, she brushed off his concern blithely. "Don't worry about it. I was so busy, I wouldn't have been able to speak to you anyway. Business has been great this week."

There was a pause, during which she wondered if Grey had discerned her insincerity. "I'm glad to hear things are going well," he finally told her. "I'm sorry I wasn't there to see you launch the new place. I'd like to make it up to you. I know it's short notice, but I'd like to take you out on Friday."

In spite of her reservations, she wanted to see him too. Almost a week had gone by since he had shown up at the store and drunk champagne with her and Sarah, and she missed him.

"Can you make it?" Grey prompted. "Say yes."

Jo smiled in surrender. "Yes."

Chapter Ten

Grey climbed tiredly from his car. His current schedule was beginning to wear on him. Ordinarily, his work with Customs at least allowed him to sleep nights, but the present case was close to being wrapped up and things were breaking fast. He'd had a late rendezvous with an unscrupulous dealer the night before, tightening the noose on the sting operation that had been months in the planning.

In addition, there was still his university work to keep up with. He loved teaching, but if he never had to look at another student's paper again, life could only get better. He had finished grading the last of the essays an hour earlier. A few caused him to wonder what the hell the kids were on.

Under the circumstances, maintaining any kind of a personal relationship was akin to keeping plates spinning in the air, but he deemed the juggling act worth the effort. Jo was the best part of his life. Just thinking about seeing her again banished the tiredness.

He pushed through the gate and crossed the courtyard to her door. Before he had a chance to ring the bell, she pulled the door open and smiled. "Hi. I heard you come in."

The sight of her was just what he needed. Looking at her filled him with an energy he hadn't known he still possessed. He leaned down and kissed her hello, careful to keep it light. His plans for the evening didn't include dragging her off to bed immediately — later maybe, but not first thing.

"Hi yourself," he said softly, straightening away from her. His gaze traveled slowly over her long black tunic sweater, black designer jeans that ended in half-boots, and back up to the chunky gold and onyx earrings. Her hair was pulled back tightly and held by a large, black bow.

"That's your idea of dressing down?"

He'd warned her dinner was going to be casual — not because he wasn't willing to take her somewhere elegant and expensive, but because it was time she started learning to let her hair down. In more ways than one. His gaze went back to the bow.

"What's wrong with this outfit?" A small crease marred her brow.

"Nothing. It's perfect. That's the

191

problem." He reached up and explored the bow until he discovered the barrette under it. He unfastened the barrette and tossed it on the foyer table behind her, then finger-combed her hair down around her shoulders. His eyes regarded her with approval. "This is better."

"Any other improvements you want to make before we go?" she asked tartly.

"None you could get away with in public."

"So you've never been to Mother's before? Somehow that doesn't surprise me." The crowded diner, catering to everyone from dockworkers to bankers, was a favorite of his. "You don't know what you've been missing. You're about to taste the best po-boy in town."

She stood in the long line beside him, her arm locked around his elbow as though afraid he might abandon her there otherwise. "It seems to be a very busy place."

"With good reason. We'll get a couple of specials and you'll see why."

The line moved quickly and they were soon seated at a table, huge sandwiches made on French bread fresh from the oven before them. Jo regarded her towering combination of ham, roast beef, shredded cabbage, and Creole mustard doubtfully, as though trying to determine how to begin.

Grey smiled and swallowed the mouthful he had been chewing, washing it down with a healthy drink of the icy beer he considered the only suitable accompaniment to one of Mother's sandwiches. "Just pick it up and dig in," he told her, amused.

She gathered the sandwich carefully in her hands and nibbled on the edges where filling extended beyond the bread.

"You could starve like that."

Her lashes lifted and she looked over the sandwich at him. "You do it your way and I'll do it mine."

Grey noticed, however, it wasn't too many minutes before she gave up trying to be neat and began enjoying the sandwich with zeal. By the time she pushed her still half-full plate away, the fingers of both hands were greasy. It was a start.

"That was delicious, but I couldn't eat another bite," she said, wiping her hands on a paper napkin. When she had as much grease off as would come, she refolded the napkin neatly and laid it beside her plate. Well, he couldn't expect her to loosen up overnight.

She took a sip of beer, then set the glass

back down and appeared absorbed by the ring of moisture it made. When she finally lifted her face, her eyes held an unfamiliar expression. "Two Customs agents came to the shop on Wednesday," she said.

He paused, then took the bite he had been about to close his teeth on. He had been aware of the agents' visit, had in fact directed it. The success of the sting operation depended on absolute secrecy. He wasn't at liberty to tell Jo about it or his role in it, regardless of her innocence, until its conclusion. That meant someone else needed to interview her.

He swallowed. "What'd they want?"

She watched him closely, her gaze never leaving his face. "They said there was a real problem right now with illegal items from overseas being smuggled through New Orleans. They wanted me to call them if I came across anything suspicious."

"What kind of items?"

"Interestingly enough, antiquities."

"And have you?"

"What?"

"Come across anything suspicious."

She looked at him silently for a beat, then her gaze dropped. "I hope not."

His instincts sharpened. "What does that mean?"

She looked back up. "Just that I wouldn't want to brush elbows with something as tawdry as smuggling. I wouldn't want to find out that someone I knew, even liked, was involved with it."

He relaxed. He had been afraid a collector might have contacted her, inadvertently drawing her into the case. "I wouldn't worry too much. Sounds like Customs is on top of things."

When she made no comment, only watched him steadily, he finally asked, "Thoughts?"

"What? Oh," she shook her head. "Just my mind wandering."

"Anywhere interesting?" He smiled provocatively, hoping to bring back their earlier easy mood.

Her answering smile was small, but real. "Not particularly."

"Definitely time to do something about that. Finish your beer and we'll go get dessert."

"Grey, I couldn't possibly eat dessert. I'm already too full."

"I didn't say anything about eating it, did I?"

She regarded him suspiciously. "Is this a cute way of saying we're going to have sex?"

"I'm planning on it, but no, that's not

what I meant. Trust me. You'll like this."
He crossed his fingers that statement was true.

"Now you've piqued my interest." She drank the last sip of beer in her glass and set it on the table. "Let's go for it."

Grey unlocked the door of his apartment, then stepped back and indicated Jo should precede him. She looked up at him and frowned. "I thought you said we weren't just going to have sex."

"God, you're suspicious. Will you just go inside. You'll see in a minute."

She tipped a last skeptical glance at him and walked in, took three steps, and stopped dead. Grey moved right behind her, watching for her reaction.

She turned slowly, taking in the apartment in silence. He had left every light in the place on, brightly illuminating the pink and white crepe-paper streamers strung from corner to corner. Where they met in the middle of the room, a huge bouquet of pink and white balloons hung suspended. A banner that stretched from one wall to the other proclaimed in fanciful pink script, "Happy Birthday, Jo."

Her gaze went to his for only a moment, before it fell on the table. He had set two

196

places with china, champagne glasses, and pink paper napkins centered prominently on the plates. Her eyes widened at the sight of the cake, frosted white with pink sugar roses circling it and two candles in the shape of the numerals two and nine on the top surrounded by more roses. The gifts stacked beside one of the plates were wrapped in more pink and white, ribbons curling wildly over them.

She walked slowly to the table and touched one of the ribbon curls tentatively. She stared at the cake in utter silence, before her gaze returned to the banner on the wall. Finally she turned to him, bewilderment in her expression.

"I don't understand. You know it's not my birthday. I was born on March fourteenth."

"I remember," he said softly. "This is for all the birthday parties you didn't have growing up. You've come to mean a lot to me. I wanted to do something for you that no one else had done."

"Oh, Grey." She looked around again, her bottom lip caught between her teeth. "I don't know what to say."

He moved to her and stroked his thumb over the lip she had bitten. "Nothing." He pressed a kiss on her mouth and straightened. "Come sit down. We'll open the champagne and cut the cake. If you're really too full for any I'll just give you a token bite."

"Not on your life. I want a whole piece. It looks so wonderful, I'll find room for it."

"Good." He pulled out her chair and seated her with a flourish, before fetching the champagne from the kitchen. After opening the bottle and pouring their glasses, he lifted his flute in a toast.

"To the little girl you were and the woman you've become." He tapped the rim of his glass against hers, causing the crystal to chime, and sipped.

"Thank you, Grey." She looked down at her plate. "Paper napkins?" She returned her gaze to his, a smile in her eyes.

"I'm making a statement."

"Saying what?"

"You're a smart girl. You figure it out." He dug in his pocket and extracted matches. "We can't cut the cake without doing the candle thing first."

He struck a match and lit the two numeral-shaped candles. "I wanted to have twenty-nine candles for the effect, but figured by the time I had them all burning the cake would be moldy. These two are standing in as tokens."

He shook out the match and dropped it on the edge of his plate. "There. Now you have to make a wish. Close your eyes. That's right. I think it's a rule or something. Got it?" She nodded. "Okay. Open your eyes and blow."

She did, easily extinguishing the flames, and laughed.

"According to legend," he told her, "your wish will now come true."

"As simple as that."

"I wouldn't put too much stock in the legend, but it can't hurt to go through the motions. What did you wish for?"

Her eyes took on a pensive cast for a moment, before the corners of her lips turned up. "I thought that was supposed to be a secret."

"Even from Prince Charming?"

"*Especially* from him."

Her eyes had gone sad again. "Okay, you're off the hook," he said. "I won't insist." He cut the cake and dumped a slice on her plate, wanting to distract her from whatever thought had troubled her.

When they finished the slices on their plates, he carried the dirty dishes into the kitchen, then refilled their champagne glasses. "Ready to open some presents?"

"Always." She started to reach for the nearest box, but he removed it from her reach.

"No. This one gets saved for last. Start with the little one."

She picked up the smallest package and shook it lightly, obviously curious. Her fingers slipped the ribbon off in the careful way he remembered and removed the paper. After lifting off the lid of the box and parting the tissue paper inside, she laughed delightedly. "However did you think of this?"

She pulled the bottle of pink bubble liquid from its tissue-paper nest and unscrewed the cap, before reaching inside for the wand. Her lips pursed and she blew a stream of iridescent bubbles in his direction.

He smiled and popped two of the bubbles with his finger. "Because it struck me as silly. Something I think you need more of."

She wrinkled her nose. "Don't preach. What's next?"

"Greedy little thing, aren't you? Here."

She reached for the next box, larger than the first had been, and hefted it in her hand, before going through the same routine as before. Grey didn't rush her, content to watch her pleasure.

Silence greeted the gift. When at last she lifted the porcelain doll from the wrapping and smiled, Grey's fear he had guessed wrong was relieved. "Every little girl ought to have a doll. I figured you hadn't had many." He thought of the assortment that had filled the shelves and sat on the beds of Sarah's and Andrea's rooms.

"None like this one." She studied it a moment longer. "Why, it looks like me."

Grey remembered seeing it in a window and knowing Jo should have it. Its blond hair and light brown eyes had brought her to mind immediately. "When they were growing up, Sarah and Andrea wanted dolls that resembled them."

"I did, too," she said quietly, gazing at the doll. "She's very special. Thank you, Grey."

"You're welcome. You can play with her later," he said taking the doll and putting her back in the box. "You have more to open."

He shoved the next to the last present in front of her, a box roughly six inches square. "Don't rattle this one or you'll break it."

She threw him a quick glance, before returning her attention to the present. "Grey, I don't know what to say. This is all too much."

"Not for twenty-nine years, it's not. Go on. Open it."

"All right, but you're making me feel terribly spoiled."

"Good. That's how you're supposed to feel on your birthday, and we're making up for a lot of them."

Jo tore the paper off, faster than with the previous gifts, Grey noted. She was forgetting to be fastidious.

"Oh, my," she breathed and carefully lifted the porcelain music box out. It was shaped like a carousel, with horses prancing around it decked out in brilliant red, blue, and green, the manes and tails streaming out behind accented with gold.

"Wind it up," he told her.

She did so and set it down on the table. The carousel revolved slowly while the strains of "Twinkle, Twinkle Little Star" issued merrily from it. Jo rolled her lips in and bit down so hard they lost color. "It's so —" She shook her head and dropped her lashes, hiding her eyes from his view.

Not fooled for a minute, he moved quickly to avert her tears. "We're down to the last one. You can't believe how much I've looked forward to seeing you in these. I kept this one for last, because I want you to put on what's in this box."

She gave a tiny sniff and smiled. "I knew

we'd get to the sex part eventually. It's lingerie, isn't it?"

"Open it and see."

When she opened the gift, her brows creased in a puzzled frown. "What . . . ?"

"Take them out of the box."

She held a bright fuzzy pink rabbit in each hand, looking from one to the other. "Slippers! You bought me slippers! I can't believe it." Her rich, throaty laugh tickled his nerve ends.

"I expect you to model those for me."

She tugged off her half-boots and nestled her feet in the ridiculous bunnies. When she had them on, she turned and held her legs straight out in front of her. "Well, is this the effect you were going for?"

His gaze took in the hair flowing casually around her shoulders and the eyes that danced above a lighthearted grin. "Absolutely."

She scissored her legs, making the rabbits' ears flop, and laughed again. "They're certainly comfortable."

"Try walking around in them."

She bounced up and paced around the living room. Grey poured himself another glass of champagne and pushed his chair away from the table, propping his ankle on his other knee to watch her. He had to grin himself, seeing the contrast her dramatic black made with the absurd pink slippers. She came back to stand before him, and rocked the toes of first one foot up and then the other.

"Hop, hop," she said, and chuckled. "They're so stupid looking, they're cute." She glanced up from her feet as a thought seemed to occur to her. "Is this another dose of silly?"

"Uh huh."

"Aren't you afraid I'll OD?"

"Not on the little bit you've had. You're still suffering from a pretty acute deficiency."

"As serious as that, huh?"

" 'Fraid so. It's going to require drastic measures."

"What do you suggest?"

He looked up at her, a smile tugging at the corner of his mouth. "There's still one part of the birthday tradition we haven't taken care of."

"What else could you possibly do, Grey? You decorated, you gave me a cake, presents. It's all really —" He watched awareness dawn and his smile widened.

"No," she said, shaking her head slowly. "No, we're not going to do that." She began to back away from him, hands crossed protectively behind her.

He set his champagne down. "Yeah, we are." He moved to stand and she spun away. Before she had taken two steps, the slippers tripped her up and she would have fallen if he hadn't caught her around her waist. She gave a laughing yelp as he swung her up and held her tightly.

"Grey, put me down! Right now." The laugh in her voice compromised the authority of her command. His grip held firm, although she landed a couple of solid hits as she kicked and pummeled.

He gave a grunt when her foot connected with his stomach. "If you hurt me," he warned, "it'll go a lot harder for you."

He dropped to the couch and turned her over his knee, anchoring her with an arm, while she alternately squealed and laughed.

He already had his hand raised, when she implored, "Wait, wait! How about if you just do a token couple of swats? You know, like the candles."

He pretended to consider for a moment. "Nope. I think we need to go for the whole twenty-nine. Don't forget, we're making up for a lot of lost time. One." His hand connected with her trim bottom in a slap, only hard enough to make noise, not really sting. Nevertheless, she yelped dramatically and tried to squirm off his lap.

"What a wuss. I thought you were made of sterner stuff," he said, bringing his hand down a second time. "Two."

"Ow. Some Prince Charming you turned out to be." Since she had trouble getting the words out through her laughter, he didn't take her comment too seriously.

By the tenth swat he was wondering how the hell he was going to finish when all he could think about was skinning her snug jeans off her wiggling butt and making love to her. Suddenly the sound of her laughter turned abruptly to sobs. Appalled, he grabbed her shoulders and hauled her upright. She knelt on the floor beside his knees, tears filling her eyes and spilling over to run down her cheeks.

"God, I'm sorry, Jo. I didn't realize I was hitting you that hard. I didn't mean for it to really hurt. I was only kidding."

"I know." She continued to hiccup and wiped at the tears, blotting her fingers on her jeans. "That's not why I'm crying."

"Clue me in then, because I don't understand at all."

"It was everything you did tonight. The whole birthday thing. No one's ever done anything as sweet for me. It just kind of all got to me suddenly."

He reached out a hand and cupped her face gently, stroking away tears with a thumb. "Maybe I should smack you around more often if it means that much to you."

His words had the desired effect. She stopped crying instantly. "Just try that again," she warned, "and you're liable to lose teeth."

"But we haven't finished." Her eyes lit, ready for battle. "Then again," he said prudently, "ten swats is probably adequate." He winked. "If it still hurts, I can kiss it and make it better."

She laughed. "You never quit, do you?"

"I hope not. Come here." He drew her up on the sofa and pulled her in close to him with an arm around her shoulders. When he leaned over, she was already halfway to meeting him.

He kissed her carefully, as gently as though she were made of spun glass. His mouth brushed her lips softly and when they parted for him, his tongue only just touched along their inner edges.

When he raised his head, there was a new expression in her eyes. Her lashes lifted and she gazed at his face, from his eyes to his mouth and back again. Her lips formed a slight smile, before she spoke quietly. "I love you, Grey."

Chapter Eleven

Grey regarded her soberly and breathed out a tired-sounding sigh. "I know," he said, his voice more gentle than she had ever heard it.

"In my entire life, I've never said that to another man."

An expression of pain flashed briefly in his eyes. "I'm honored."

"You're supposed to say, 'I love you too, Jo.'" She fought to keep her voice light, to keep the quaver from it.

Grey removed his arm from around her shoulders and leaned forward, elbows on his knees. He closed his eyes and pressed a finger between his brows, as though his head hurt. "I knew this would come," he said. "I can't. Not again."

"Can't what. Say it or love me?"

He dropped his hands between his knees and looked over his shoulder at her. "I don't know. Either. Both. Does it matter?"

Jo thought about that. She thought about the loving way Grey had always treated her, his compassion and innate kindness. Vivian had tried to warn her, but

Grey's experience with his ex-wife had left him more crippled than even Vivian realized. Grey's problem wasn't that he was incapable of loving again, it was that he *believed* he was.

"Tell me about your marriage, Grey. You never even mention it."

The quick look he shot her told her she had surprised him. He had probably expected more tears. "It's not something I like to talk about." His terse voice announced clearly that he didn't intend to then either.

His words silenced her for a moment. Then she decided she had everything to gain and nothing to lose by pushing. "That's not fair."

He cocked an eyebrow in question.

"I have no secrets from you, Grey. Not a one. You made me tell you things no one else in the world knows about me. The telling was painful, and you knew it, dammit, but you made me do it anyway."

He frowned, whether in remorse or irritation, she couldn't be sure. There was nothing to be done at that point but plow on. "But you know something? You were right. Talking about it was like lancing a boil. It let the poison out, it brought it up to my conscious mind where I could finally start to deal with the hurt, finally start to heal. Before, I had kept all the bad stuff tamped down in my subconscious, where I thought I would be able to ignore it. Instead, that old pain was festering and poisoning my whole system."

She had his attention. He listened to her words like he was memorizing them.

"If you won't tell me about your marriage for your own sake, you owe it to me out of fairness. I bared my soul for you. You owe me at least a peek at yours."

A ghost of his usual lopsided smile touched his lips. "I suppose you have a point." He clasped his hands together, studied the knuckles. "Missy and I went to high school together. She was everything, a sixteen-year-old boy dreams about — pretty, popular, and two steps ahead of me sexually. When we were freshman, she only went out with seniors. By the time we were seniors she was dating college types. She barely noticed me, but I was happy just to breathe the same air Missy did."

He directed a wry glance at her. "I can't tell you the number of wet dreams I had in which Missy was the star."

He returned to studying his hands, flexing his fingers in silence. Jo waited for him to continue, not wanting to interrupt his thoughts. "I didn't see too much of her during college. She went off to finishing school. The year I was a senior her father lost everything because of gambling debts and she was forced to come home from her expensive school. To my surprised delight, I seemed to have become the only man Missy wanted."

Grey went on quietly and his story paralleled the one Vivian had told her, but with a few exceptions. Vivian hadn't been able to tell her how embarrassed the young Grey had been about his naiveté, how disillusioned and hurt he had been when Missy revealed her true motives, how unforgiving of himself he was for what he viewed as his own foolishness.

"There was no depth to Missy, but then she never pretended to have any. If I hadn't been wearing rose-colored glasses I would have seen Missy for the person she really was. She made no effort to be otherwise. Most other people knew not to expect anything more from her."

"But not you."

"You got that right. The whole disaster of our marriage was as much my fault as hers. I didn't want to accept what my better judgment was trying to tell me. I kept trying to force her into the mold of the woman I believed her to be. I think she was relieved when I found out about her indiscretions."

Grey fell silent and Jo wished she had a way to comfort the young man he had been. Grey had forgiven Missy, but Jo damned her for leaving Grey so doubtful of his own feelings and judgments.

She reached out and laid her hand against his back, glad when he didn't shrug it off. The muscles under her palm flexed with the deep breath he drew. "Are we even now?" he asked.

She thought about the way he had plumbed her feelings, the way he had forced her to tell him her desires the first time they made love. "Not quite, but it's a start."

He made no response and they sat that way for several minutes more, Grey staring at the floor while Jo watched his shoulders rise and fall with his breathing.

Grey finally straightened and glanced at her feet. "Take the slippers off and put your boots on. I'll take you home," he said, his voice dispirited. "I imagine that's what you want."

If she let him take her home in his present frame of mind, he would come back and brood. That didn't bode well for her or their relationship.

"I don't think it's very polite of you to tell the guest of honor that she has to leave her own birthday party."

Grey had already stood and was waiting for her to do likewise. He frowned down at her, obviously puzzled. "Jo?"

"I've never had a birthday party, Grey. I don't think I'm quite ready for it to be over."

He drew his head back, a frown pulling his brows together. "Jo, what the hell are you doing?"

She stood and stepped around him on her way to the table. "At the moment, having another glass of champagne."

He crossed his arms over his chest and she felt his gaze on her as she first poured her own glass and then refreshed his. "Would you like another piece of cake while I'm here?" she asked lightly.

Grey's gaze hadn't shifted. "No, I do not want a piece of the damn cake. I want an explanation for your behavior."

His tone told her he would brook no pretense of misunderstanding his question. She faced him squarely, feeling ridiculous having the conversation wearing enormous pink rabbits on her feet. "Wait a minute. I need a time out."

His jaw went slack, before she bent to remove the slippers. She placed the rabbits in their box and turned back to him. "Now I'm ready."

The hard line of his mouth softened into something suspiciously like a smile. "I'm waiting," he said evenly.

"What did you think, Grey — that I would tuck my tail between my legs and go home crying because you wouldn't profess your love for me?" At the guilty flush that stole up his neck, she knew that was exactly what he had thought. "I don't scare off that easily."

"Apparently not."

"I love you. That's not a weakness on my part. I'm not embarrassed about it. It doesn't make me less of a person. What it does make me, is very hard to get rid of. You don't think you can love me. Fine. Whatever."

"Jo, can I —"

"Shut up. I'm not done yet."

He held his palms up in acquiescence and nodded for her to continue.

"Together we're good, Grey. I don't care whether you want to call it love, friendship, or just convenience. I'm not hung up on the words." Hearing her lie, she suddenly ran out of steam.

She swallowed and said in a voice braver than she felt, "I think we should just let things ride and see where they take us." If he gave her a no, she hoped she could keep from begging.

"That isn't really what you want, Jo."

"Depends on what the other options are."

"There aren't any," he said, his voice level.

"That's what I thought. Then that *is* what I want." She picked up both glasses of champagne and crossed to Grey. "Here."

When he had taken his glass from her, she raised hers. "*I* want to propose a toast. To birthday parties." She tapped her glass against his and drank. "What's a girl have to do to get laid at one?"

Grey set his glass on the coffee table with an abrupt clink. "I should have spanked you harder." His hands grasped her shoulders and gave her a shake. He ignored her yelp as champagne sloshed over her hand. "I have never 'laid' you as you so elegantly put it. I *have* made love to you and would like to do so again if you'd be quiet long enough. Although at the moment, the thought of warming your bottom holds more appeal."

"Sounds kinky." She had hit a nerve. There was hope. She licked champagne off her hand, then tipped up her glass and drank what was left in it.

Grey blew out a laugh in obvious exasperation. "What am I going to do with you?"

"Is that a rhetorical question, or are you asking for hints?"

"Don't help me. I want to do it on my own."

"While you think about it, I'm going to get a refill." She turned to go to the table, but his hand stopped her.

"No, you're not. You've had enough." He plucked her glass from her fingers. "And you won't need this any longer. I've just figured out what to do with you."

Jo moaned under his hands and reached to touch him in return. His loving was different somehow that night. His hands and mouth moved slowly, almost worshipfully over her, igniting small fires wherever they lighted and leaving her gasping. He had brought her to arousal so gradually, so gently she could have wept with the beauty of it.

He laved a nipple with his tongue, then blew softly. His cooling breath burned straight to her core and she inhaled sharply. His lips brushed back and forth over the erect bud, eliciting a whimper from her. When his teeth gnawed tenderly, she arched high, craving more.

He continued for what felt like hours, unhurried in spite of her pleas, leaving no inch of her body unloved, unaroused. He led her to the edge repeatedly, never quite letting her cross. Each time he would draw her back gently, soothing her with whispered caresses, before driving her up again.

The tension coiling inside her had become unbearable. "Please, Grey, please," she begged, desperate for his possession. "No more. I need you." Her arms reached to bring him down to her.

At last he moved between her thighs and she opened them wider, wanting him inside quickly. Even then he made her wait, taking her with excruciating slowness, although she felt what the effort cost him in the quivering of his muscles. When he was buried deep, she arched her pelvis up and exploded in a paroxysm of pleasure, sobbing with the intensity of it.

Afterwards, his arms cradled her against his chest, and she lay contentedly, eyes closed. He may not have given her the words, but he had shown her his love. She slept, exhausted by the emotional roller coaster of the evening.

When she opened her eyes groggily, daylight speared through the blinds and Grey stood in front of the mirror, looping a tie around his neck.

"Grey?"

He glanced at her reflection in the mirror and smiled as he tied the knot. "Good morning. I was going to leave you a note before I left. I've got my Saturday class this morning, but that's no reason why you should have to get up. Go back to sleep. I'll be back in a couple of hours." His smile took on a provocative gleam. "I'd love to come home to you still in my bed."

"If you're trying to kill me, there are easier ways to do it."

"Yeah, but not nearly as much fun." He picked up change and keys off the dresser, shoved them into his pockets, and turned from the mirror. "Seriously, honey, I know you're stuck here until I get back. Make yourself at home. There are spare toothbrushes in the cupboard under the sink in the guest bathroom. The paper's on the kitchen counter and there's coffee in the pot when you're ready. Help yourself to whatever you can find to eat. I'll get back as soon as I can."

"I can take a taxi home, Grey. You don't need to hurry back for me."

He opened the closet door and took his

bomber jacket off a hanger. "I want to." Bending over the bed he planted a quick kiss on her mouth, before straightening and checking his watch. "See you soon."

The apartment door slammed shut before she had come fully awake. She burrowed under the covers again, deciding going back to sleep had been a good idea. When she woke for the second time, she drew her arm from beneath the sheet to look at her watch and was surprised to see she had slept for an hour. She had intended to just close her eyes for a few minutes.

Waking in a bed other than her own felt strange. The few times in the past she had had sex she had insisted on going home afterward. Actually sleeping beside someone had seemed too threatening. It left you too vulnerable. With Grey, none of the old fears had even come up.

She stretched her muscles awake, before sliding from beneath the covers and padding into the bathroom. Grey had told her to make herself at home and she would start by using his shower.

After scrubbing her skin until it glowed pink and shampooing her hair, she stepped from the stall and dried off with one of the towels hanging from the rack, before wrapping it turban-style around her head. The bathrobe of Grey's she had worn previously hung on a hook on the back of the door and she made use of it again. Although it was much too big, rolling the sleeves up and pulling the belt tight helped.

The robe smelled faintly of Grey's aftershave and his own indefinable scent. She closed her eyes and inhaled, hugging herself, loving the intimacy of wearing something that had been next to Grey's skin. After quickly brushing her teeth with the toothbrush she found where Grey had promised, she headed for the kitchen and the coffee whose aroma had been teasing her for the past several minutes.

She dumped cornflakes, the only breakfast offering she could find, into a bowl, poured coffee into a mug and carried both along with *The Times-Picayune* to the dining table. Saving the front page until she had fortified herself with food and coffee, she turned to the society section and spent an enjoyable few minutes lost in the city's preparations for upcoming Mardi Gras.

The ringing of the telephone startled her from the world of krewes, costumes, floats, and feuds. She wondered if she ought to pick it up, but hesitated. Answering Grey's phone seemed presumptuous. She noted his answering machine was on and decided to let it take the call.

She heard Grey's recorded directions and then the voice of the caller. "This is J.D. I got the item you were interested in. Call me to arrange a meeting."

The message ended abruptly with no good-bye or further information. There had been something about that voice. Jo tried to shrug off the call and go back to the newspaper, but something kept nagging at her. Finally she gave up on following society's doings.

With the vague sense that she was violating Grey's privacy, she hit the play button. Frowning in concentration as she listened to the voice again, she tried to pin down the familiarity of it. Where had she heard that hoarse, too-many-cigarettes tone before?

Joseph DeLong. She hadn't seen him in two years, but she remembered the local antique dealer who spoke out of the side of his mouth. His demeanor more resembled that of a used car salesman. There had been rumors a year or so earlier that he had been caught selling fakes. Nothing had ever been proven, though.

That Grey had any business at all with

the man was disturbing. The evening before had driven all thought of her suspicions from mind, but now they rushed back, full force. The evidence, circumstantial though it might be, that Grey was involved in something unsavory was piling up. She rinsed her dishes pensively and loaded them into the dishwasher, before going to dress.

She combed out her hair and made do with the few cosmetics in her purse. After making the bed, she poured herself a second cup of coffee and paced the apartment waiting for Grey. At the case holding the frankincense container, she stopped and stared, brows knit. If only the thing could talk.

Grey walked in and saw her, standing in front of the frankincense container, and his gaze made a quick journey of her body. "You're dressed. Too bad. Still, we can fix that."

"Another time, Grey. I'm behind on paperwork and Miriam, my weekend help, wants to leave early today."

She had spoken too quickly. His eyes narrowed as he studied her. The hand around her coffee mug was grasping it so tightly her knuckles shone white. The silence reverberated between them louder than words. "Okay," he said, after a moment. "Come on. Pack up your gifts. I'll take you home now."

"You had a call. You might want to listen to the message before we leave."

Something was definitely up. He shot a questioning look at Jo before striding impatiently to the answering machine. At the sound of DeLong's voice, he cut his gaze to her, wondering what she had made of the call. He didn't like that she had heard it, hadn't wanted any of the current case he worked on to touch her.

"Nothing important," he said offhandedly. "It can wait. Let's go." He was in as big a hurry now as Jo had professed to be. He had a lot to arrange in just a very few days.

He maneuvered the Mustang through the maze of one-way streets in the Quarter, discarding one idea after the other. By the time he pulled up behind Jo's house he wasn't pleased with what was left, but could think of no other way to insure his present case didn't spill over into her life.

He shifted into park, but left the engine running. "I forgot to tell you, Jo, I'll be out of town for the next week. I leave tomorrow, as a matter of fact."

She had been retrieving her purse and boxes from the floor of the car. At his words, she straightened abruptly and looked at him in surprise. "Sudden, isn't it? Where are you going?"

At the suspicious note in her voice, he smiled blandly. "I'm presenting a paper at a conference in Atlanta. It's been scheduled for months. I meant to tell you earlier."

"What's your paper about?" Her tone challenged more than questioned. Did she think to trip him up?

"Ancient peoples of the Fertile Crescent." He had actually given the paper at a conference two years ago.

"Oh." His answer seemed to mollify her. "Well, good luck. When will you be back?"

"I'm not sure. There's an aunt and a couple of cousins in the area I intend to look up. I'll give you a call when my schedule is firmed up and let you know for sure." He made to lean over and kiss her, but she eluded him, sliding from the car quickly.

"I'll wait to hear from you then. Goodbye." She shut the door behind her and hurried to the gate, leaving him to wonder over her uncharacteristic behavior.

Chapter Twelve

Grey had been gone the better part of a week, but he was with Jo as surely as though he walked by her side. Thoughts of him accompanied her constantly. Was he guilty, and if so, of what exactly? The logical half of her brain said yes, of course. Look at the evidence. The emotional half reminded her he was the good and honorable man she was in love with.

And hadn't she always believed when she finally found her Prince Charming that he would carry her off on his white horse to live happily ever after? Where was it written that they rode off to his castle and played house? Being with Grey was becoming increasingly painful for Jo. She wanted so much more and Grey shut down at even the thought.

She pressed her fingers against her temple, trying to massage away the headache forming there, as her boot heels thumped hollowly on the wooden boardwalk of the waterfront. The freighter containing her shipment from Boston had docked earlier, and she wanted to insure that the items she had purchased on her buying trip had arrived safely. She also needed to make arrangements for their delivery.

Jo located the shipping agent amidst the men working loudly at a myriad of activities. She ignored the few whistles and comments on her anatomy. The waterfront was familiar territory to her.

Raising his voice to be heard above the sound of water traffic, forklifts, and coarse human conversation, the agent assured her her shipment had been on the cargo manifest and had already been unloaded. The wooden crates currently waited in the dockside warehouse for pickup. He directed Jo to their location and she thanked him, before moving carefully around men and machinery to inspect her cargo.

The crates appeared to be in good shape, with no major dents or dinged corners, so presumably the contents had arrived unscathed. She hunted up the warehouse supervisor and arranged to have the items delivered to the store, grateful to be finished. The noise in the warehouse had exacerbated her headache.

Back outside, she massaged at her temple again and inhaled deeply of the air laden with the scents of water, fish, creosote, and diesel fuel. Her gaze traveled absently over the stretch of river before her and the piers that extended into it like the fingers of a hand, before sharpening abruptly at the sight of a man two piers down.

She tried to tell herself he was too far away for a positive identification, that lately she saw him everywhere, but she knew. His build, his stance, his posture were too dear, too familiar for a mistake.

Grey stood in profile, speaking to two individuals dressed in suits, who looked glaringly out of place among the active men on the pier in work clothes. Grey himself wore old jeans that even from a distance Jo could see were torn at the knee and a pale blue work shirt. After another minute's conversation, the three men turned and boarded the ship tied up behind them.

Jo had seen more than enough. Grey had lied to her, had lied about being at a conference in Atlanta, about looking up relatives there. He had been in New Orleans all along doing God knew what. The betrayal seared deeply.

When Jo arrived home she realized she had no memory of the drive there. Her body had performed automatically when her mind shut down to protect itself from further injury. She stumbled inside, still blessedly anesthetized, but she knew the numbness couldn't last. When it wore off she wondered how she would stand the pain.

She called Miriam at the store and asked her to stay until closing that day. Business taken care off, she dropped into the first chair she came to, at a loss as to what to do with herself. She didn't know the standard procedure when dreams were irrevocably shattered.

Three hours later dusk was claiming the corner where she sat when the telephone rang. She stared blankly at the instrument, as though unsure of its use. Answering it seemed to be the only way to silence its strident ringing.

She picked up the receiver and murmured, "Hello?"

"Jo? It's Grey. I called the store and Miriam told me you were home with a headache. Must be a bad one. You don't sound so good."

Not surprising. "How was your trip?"

"Fine. I'll be back tomorrow and tell you about it then."

"And how is your aunt?" She marveled that he didn't hear the sarcasm.

"Who?"

"The aunt you were going to look up."

"Oh, her. Fine. Listen, I'll tell you all about it tomorrow. What time can I see you?"

She knew then her decision had already been made, that the only possible course of action had already presented itself. "Can you meet me at the store before closing, say four-thirty?"

"Sounds good. I'll see you then. I hope your headache is better soon, honey."

She closed her eyes at the endearment. "Good-bye."

She rose to retrieve her purse and search out the card the Customs agent had left with her. By the time she punched in the numbers from it, her hands were shaking. In only a few moments she was speaking with Brannigan himself.

"This is Jo Flaherty of Empress Antiques. You asked me to call if I came across anything suspicious regarding the smuggling of illegal antiquities."

His answer was a cautious, "Yes?"

"It has come to my attention that someone I know is very much involved in the activity, may even be one of the key players." She struggled to keep her voice even.

Several seconds of silence greeted her

announcement. "What makes you think so?" Brannigan finally asked.

Jo detailed the evidence she had observed.

"I see. What is the name of this individual?"

"I . . . would rather not say. He's coming to my store tomorrow afternoon. Could you meet us there at five o'clock, closing time?"

"If your suspicions are correct, Miss Flaherty, you could be in some danger. For your own protection, you should give me the person's name."

"I'll be safe." Whatever else Grey might be guilty of, he would never knowingly hurt her. Of that, she was sure. "Can you come?"

"We'll be there." Jo could hear his impatience with her. "Thank you for your call."

Relief at having the investigation concluded and the key figures involved in custody lightened his mood and his steps as he walked into Empress Antiques. He was looking forward to being able to share with Jo the other half of his life. The past few months had been a grind he was glad to see the end of.

Jo sat at her desk, her attention centered on the papers there, but at his entrance her head came up sharply. She stood, her movements jerky, and remained behind the desk. Grey frowned, puzzled by the expression she wore. He had expected a hello hug, had been counting on one, but Jo made no move toward him. Her face was white, her mouth pinched.

He approached her and put his hand on her shoulder, before kissing her. For the first time in his memory her lips didn't soften for him. If anything they became even tighter.

He straightened, his eyes questioning. "I've missed you." His gaze searched her face warily. "You're pale. Is your head still bothering you?"

"My head is fine."

"Then what's wrong?"

She looked down and rearranged the papers on her desk.

"Talk to me, Jo."

Her gaze lifted to his and the anguish in her expression shocked him. "Why, Grey? Why did you do it? Was it the money? Was it just too easy to resist?"

Her words took him aback. "What the hell are you talking about?"

"You know what I'm talking about. The smuggling. I'm afraid you can't pretend with me any longer, Grey. I've suspected for a long time, and now I know."

"You think I'm involved in smuggling?" He

was incredulous. Had the woman lost her mind? "Where did you get an idea like that?"

"I saw you on the pier yesterday when you were supposed to be in Atlanta."

He latched onto the only piece of information that made any sense to him. "You were on the pier? I didn't see you there."

"The point is *I* saw *you*."

"And on the basis of that you decided I was a smuggler? How do you account for the other several hundred people a day who have occasion to be at the docks?"

"But you lied to me."

"With good reason."

"There were other things, too, that pointed at your being guilty."

"Like what?"

If Jo weren't so obviously upset, the irony of the situation would be laughable. She actually suspected him of committing the crimes he had been investigating for the past eight months. After planning on being able to finally tell her about the case and receive well-deserved congratulations for a job well done, instead he stood accused.

Her gaze veered to the small French clock on her desk. "We're running out of time. They'll be here in a few minutes."

"Who will?"

"Customs. They're coming to arrest you,

Grey." Her hands squeezed each other, the fingers knotting together.

He couldn't prevent the bark of laughter that escaped. "This I'd like to see." The afternoon was turning into a farce.

"How can you laugh? It's more serious than you think. I told them about the things in your apartment, about the frankincense container, the mysterious phone calls. The money hidden under your dresser."

"How did you — never mind. It's not important now. Did you give them my name?" He could imagine the reaction at headquarters. They were probably bent double over that one.

"No, but they'll find you eventually, anyway. There's still time to turn yourself in. Surely you'd get some kind of credit for that. And turning state's evidence against the others involved would buy you leniency. Please, Grey. It's your only hope."

"What about everything you know? Your testimony could be pretty damning."

She thought for a moment, and then her eyes widened. "I know. You can marry me. As soon as you get out on bail, we can have it done. Then I can't be forced to testify against you. It'll work." Her gaze flew excitedly to his. "It'll work, Grey."

The situation was no longer funny. Jo

was sincere and her generosity almost brought him to his knees. All her life she had dreamed of having a family and respectability. She had just offered to give them both up for his sake. Had anyone ever loved him so much?

"Honey, I can't let you do that," he said softly.

"It's okay, honestly. I know it won't be a real marriage. We can get a divorce as soon as you're acquitted."

This had gone on long enough. "Jo, there's something you don't —"

At the sound of the door, they both turned. Agents Brannigan and Kernan entered and looked surprised to find Grey there ahead of them.

"Grey," Brannigan said. "What are you doing here? I thought you were going home to a much needed rest. Brian and I are supposed to be cleaning up the loose ends."

"You know Mr. Cantrell?" Jo asked Brannigan, her shock evident.

"Yes, he —"

"I seem to be one of those loose ends, Ted. I'm the person you were called to meet," Grey interrupted, before Brannigan could complete his sentence.

"You're kidding."

"Don't say anything more, Grey, until you get a lawyer here," Jo advised.

Wide grins split the agents' faces. "Miss Flaherty," Brannigan began, "Grey Cantrell is —"

"Is telling you to leave," Grey said. "I'll straighten everything out at headquarters later. Tell them it was a false alarm."

"Sure thing, Grey." Brannigan gave him a slight nod, signaling understanding. The agents bid Jo farewell, grins still firmly in place, and Grey knew it would be a long time before he heard the last of this one.

Jo locked the door behind them and looked at him, her face a blank. "What just happened here?"

"It's a long story." And technically, he wasn't free to tell her all of it.

She crossed her arms. "I've got time."

Rules needed bending occasionally. "Well . . ." Grey recounted the story, from the first appearance locally of the smuggled antiquities, to his involvement, and the sting operation just the night before that captured the ring-leader and those next-in-line. The smaller operators were being arrested as testimony exposed them.

"But what about the artifacts in your apartment?" Jo asked.

"Just what I said they were — reproductions, except for the frankincense container that was a gift."

"And the cash?"

"Government money used to convince dealers I was a bona fide buyer. I purchased a number of smaller items to set them up for bigger sales. How did you find that, by the way?"

"Looking for a lost earring."

Grey reflected wryly that it was sometimes the littlest things that felled kingdoms.

"Why couldn't you tell me what you were doing?" Jo asked plaintively.

"The success of the operation depended on absolute secrecy. Not even Vivian knows I work for Customs."

"And now that I do, I guess you'll have to kill me, right?"

"I liked your first idea better."

"Which one was that?"

"I think I should marry you."

"Don't joke about it, Grey. I must have sounded ridiculous to you, but I was serious."

"I know you were," he said gently. "I am too. If I had any doubts about the reality of your love, they were taken care of when you offered to marry a criminal and live under a cloud of suspicion to save his sorry hide. I'm ashamed it took that kind of proof to convince me."

He expected an exuberant hug, but she surprised him again. She tipped her head to one side and asked gravely, "Do you love me?"

He closed his eyes and sighed deeply, before opening them again and meeting her direct gaze. "Yes. And if that's not the hardest thing I've ever said, I don't know what is."

"Why is it so hard?"

"Because I'm rusty. I haven't said it in a long time. Haven't wanted to, haven't dared to. Handing over your heart is a pretty scary thing."

Her eyes shone with tears. "I promise I'll take good care of it."

"I know. You already have." He pulled her to him and kissed her with a tenderness he hadn't known he possessed. "So will you?"

"What?"

"Marry me?"

"Before or after you make love to me again?"

"After," he said, eyeing the big brass bed that still reposed grandly in the store. "Definitely after."